"Katy Morgan is a richly
brings her gifts to bear o
short narrative ever written as she sensitively, faithfully and imaginatively retells the biblical story of Ruth and Naomi. Drawn into the twists and turns of their emotion-packed world, we marvel at God's faithful care and by the end discover where their story will eventually lead. While written with young people in mind, I suspect *The Outsider* will be read and enjoyed by those of every age!"

SINCLAIR B. FERGUSON, Chancellor's Professor of Systematic
Theology, RTS; Author, *The Whole Christ* and *Faithful God:
The Wisdom of God's Sovereignty in the Book of Ruth*

"A wonderful retelling of a beautiful story. Katy draws us into the drama and helps us feel the tension, fear, loss and despair of Ruth and Naomi—and their rising hope of a redeemer. The Lord's kindness and sovereign care for his people shines through each chapter, fuelling the reader's desire to know his love and protection themselves. Younger and older readers alike will be enthralled from start to finish."

CAROLYN LACEY, Women's Worker,
Woodgreen Evangelical Church, Worcester; Author,
(Extra)Ordinary Hospitality and *Say the Right Thing*

"Katy Morgan invites readers into the world of Ruth and Naomi, enriching our understanding of God's unwavering kindness and faithfulness to his people through their story. This engaging retelling of the book of Ruth helps children to understand and connect with God's word in a fresh and poignant way."

WHITNEY NEWBY, Founder, Brighter Day Press;
Author, *Lift Your Eyes*

THE OUTSIDER

RUTH: A RETELLING

KATY MORGAN

thegoodbook
COMPANY

Katy Morgan is the award-winning author of *Songs of a Warrior* and a Senior Editor at The Good Book Company. She likes climbing hills and exploring new places—both in books and in real life! Before Katy joined TGBC, she used to work in a school, and now she teaches the Bible every week to children at her church. She also reads ancient Greek and has a master's degree in Classics from Cambridge University.

The Outsider
© The Good Book Company, 2025

Published by:
The Good Book Company

thegoodbook

COMPANY

thegoodbook.com | thegoodbook.co.uk
thegoodbook.com.au | thegoodbook.co.nz | thegoodbook.co.in

Cover illustration by Megan Parker | Internal illustrations by Alex Webb-Peploe
Design and Art Direction by André Parker

ISBN: 9781802542974 | JOB-008021| Printed in India

Contents

For Sarah

Unto you is born this day in the city of David
a Saviour, which is Christ the Lord.

THE LAND OF ISRAEL

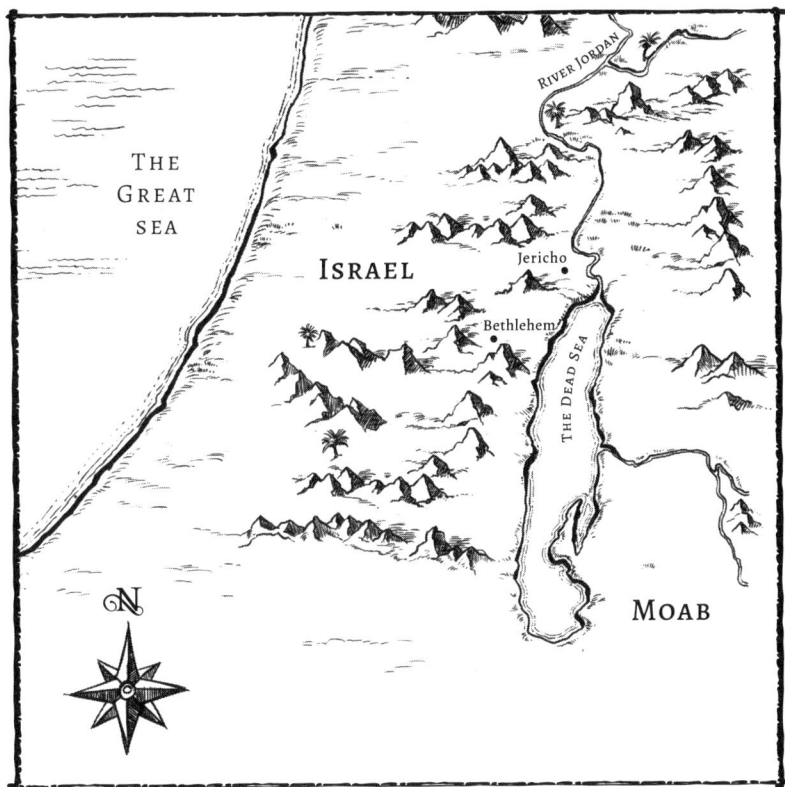

This map is full of real places because the story you're about to read is based on a true one, found in the book of Ruth in the Old Testament part of the Bible. If at any stage you want to know more about the history that lies behind this book, turn to page 159—there are accompanying notes for each chapter.

CHAPTER 1

The Decision

My mother-in-law's mouth was as wrinkled as a prune. Right then she was pursing her lips, so the deep grooves around them were especially obvious. I think she'd pursed them too many times, and they'd got stuck that way.

Her forehead was furrowed as well. Her eyes were fierce.

"Go home," she said again. "You are *not* coming with me."

But I shook my head. Naomi wasn't going to have her way this time.

I looked back. Orpah was already a dark figure disappearing in the half-grown barley. It was just after dawn, and the light was still low, making my friend's shadow long and black as she walked back towards our village.

My mother-in-law interpreted my backwards glance as hesitation. "Go with her," she said insistently. "Go back to your own people. Go home."

But I stood my ground.

I didn't care that Naomi was much older than me. I didn't care that I was supposed to do what she said.

It was for her own good.

I pursed my lips just like her.

"*Don't* urge me to leave you," I said. "*Don't* urge me to turn back."

The lines around Naomi's mouth deepened. I put my hand on her arm, wishing I could get across everything I was feeling.

"Where you go," I said firmly, "I will go."

I stared at her.

She stared at me.

***

The day I first saw Naomi was ten years before that—it was the day my third sister was born. I was twelve years old, and I had woken early that morning to find myself being shooed out of the house by my aunts.

"Ruth, get up!" one of them shouted at me. "The baby is coming!"

She was pulling the blankets away from where they'd twisted around my body in sleep. My other aunt forced my hand open and shoved a chunk of bread into it, then yanked me upright. "No place for you here," she said, flapping at me to tell me to go. "Out!"

I shook my head slowly, still sleepy. "I'm old enough. I should stay with Ma."

"Out, out!" the aunts cried again, in unison this time. "Take your brother with you. Reminah and Amam have already gone."

I looked down at my sisters' empty bed on the ground. Usually we had to pile up the bedrolls and fold the blankets neatly each morning to make space for everything else the room was used for during the day. But now Reminah and Amam's blankets lay in a crumpled heap, just like mine.

Bek, the youngest and the only boy, was crouched in a corner sucking his thumb. His eyes were big as he watched my aunts. I held out my hand, and he grabbed my fingers in his small, slobbery fist.

"Ugh," I said, and swung him up onto my hip instead.

"Out," said the nearest aunt again, but she was distracted this time. Deep groans were coming from the tiny room where my parents slept. The new baby really was on its way.

"Out!" My aunt gave me a little shove and then hurried out of the room.

Obediently, I held Bek tight and headed in the opposite direction.

The sunlight took me by surprise: I blinked and stepped back for a moment, losing my balance and making my brother bang his head on my shoulder. The goat snickered at me from her position tethered to a tree just outside the house.

I wrinkled my nose back at her. "The joke's on you," I said, sticking my tongue out. *I* was the one who was free to go wherever I wanted for once. I hardly ever got sent out of the house like this without some sort of errand. Nobody would want me back for hours now that my aunts had taken over, and when I really thought about it, I definitely *didn't* want to be around for the birth. But what to do with a day of freedom?

First I had to do something with Bek, who was now getting his slimy fingers all over my hair. I put him down hurriedly. "You need looking after for the day, don't you? Hmm. I know. How about we go and see Dinah?"

"Di," he answered cheerfully. And so on we toddled across the village.

It was a small place, our village. Just a bunch of mud-brick houses scraped together in a loose circle. Our house sat on the top of a low rise of ground from which you could see for miles across the wide, flat plain of Moab. Everything felt fresh and good that morning, now that I'd got used to being awake; the sun was shining, the cold weather was behind us, and the spring rains had made everything green. The houses looked snug and neat in the early sunshine.

Except the house next to ours. That belonged to the widow Zowelah, and it was dirty and crumbling. As Bek and I dawdled past, I noticed that the long cracks in one of its walls had tiny pink and white flowers growing in them.

"Fla," said Bek (meaning "flowers"). He reached towards them, but I dragged him away. I was sure those cracks were getting wider.

***

We found Dinah sitting on a stool in the little courtyard outside her house. She was twisting a fuzz of wool around one end of a long stick, ready to spin it into yarn—but she set it down as I came near and lifted her cheek so that I could kiss her.

"Ma is giving birth right now," I said. "My aunts are there."

Dinah nodded. "She'll be well, then. A strong woman, anyway, your mother."

Bek was reaching out his chubby hands to be lifted onto her lap. She helped him up. "*Your* arrival didn't give her much trouble, did it, Bek-boy? So this new baby won't either."

I shuddered. Bek's birth had sounded like quite a lot of trouble to me.

"We must pray that it will be another boy," Dinah added, nodding towards the shrine that stood in the opposite corner of her courtyard.

"We've been praying that every day," I told her. "*Please, great gods, give us a healthy, strong boy, who will keep the family line going and look after our parents in their old age.* We've said it every single day."

"Good girl," Dinah smiled. "Now, I suppose you're not welcome at home for a while? I just sent Orpah off to the well, and she has work to do after she comes back. But if you help her for a while, I think I can spare her for the rest of the morning." She raised her eyebrows knowingly. "*And* I can keep Bek with me."

Bek said, "Di," enthusiastically.

So that was that. Soon I was running to find Orpah—Dinah's daughter, and my best friend.

And it was during that morning of freedom that we would first meet Naomi.

CHAPTER 2

The Strangers

Orpah and I wandered down through the fields, where the barley stalks were now well above ankle height.

"Race you," I shouted as soon as we reached the first field boundary. "To the last marker!"

"We're not allowed to go that far—" Orpah stuttered after me, but I was already flying, my arms outstretched like a bird's wings.

"Come on!" I called. "I'm leaving you behind!" And with satisfaction I heard her sandals begin to thump hard against the earth as she took on speed. Orpah had longer legs than me, but I was almost as fast as her, and with my head start, I thought I could win.

I was laughing, grinning. The air and the green barley and the sun in the sky were like one big gulp of cool delicious water. My hastily braided hair was coming undone, but I didn't mind. Orpah was still behind me, and my mother and aunts were even further away; nobody could tell me what to do… I was free.

I'd passed two boundary markers already, and there was the final one ahead of me: a big chunk of grey stone that looked like a crouching man with a hood over his head. Sometimes people left offerings to the gods on it—a jug of oil or a grain-cake, perched on its flat top like a hat. But not today.

I'd always wanted to touch that boundary stone. We weren't supposed to go as far as this, it was true. We were out of sight of most of the village. Dinah would have said that we were running the risk of being outside the protection of the village gods. But personally, I'd never seen what there was to be scared of. I was nearly there now, and Orpah was getting close behind me. I grunted, forcing my legs to go faster. I wanted to win!

Orpah gave a sudden shriek. "Ruth!"

"Don't… put me… off!" I panted, pushing myself forwards—then I shrieked too.

The stone was moving.

I skidded to a halt, lost my footing and crashed to the dusty ground.

"Ruth!" cried Orpah again, catching up. Her hands scrabbled at me as she pulled me to my feet.

"The stone—" I said, spinning round to look at it again—

"They're *strangers*," she hissed, clutching me.

And so they were.

The marker hadn't moved. Someone had stirred behind it. Another someone by its side. Their grey cloaks had made them blend in with the stone. But now we could see them: four of them, four strangers, four complete strangers right in front of us.

Orpah and I took a step back.

The closest was a man, straightening up now and towering over us. His grey hair was covered with a faded cap. Next to him were two boys, both tall, both very thin. They were staring at us.

And then there was her.

Naomi's billowing dress hid the thinness of her body, but her face was bony, and her lips were cracked. She must have been very hungry and very exhausted. Yet even then, even that first time I met her, those sharp eyes were looking us up and down, and those lips were pursed in disapproval.

Instinctively I straightened my dusty clothes and smoothed my loose hair back behind my ears.

"So these are Moabites," Naomi said crisply.

Her husband sighed. His sigh turned into a cough, and he bent double for a moment, his whole body jerking with the effort his lungs were making.

Orpah moved a little closer to me.

Naomi's expression was softening, though. She rubbed her husband's back, helping him to straighten up as the coughing fit came to an end. Then she looked at us again. "Girls," she said slowly, "we're very hungry. We're looking for work, and a place to live. Does your village have room for us?"

Her words sounded strange. She wasn't from Moab, that was for sure. Was she Ammonite, like the traders who came from the north sometimes and bought dried herbs and flowers from Dinah? Was she a nomad from the south?

"We are Ephrathites, from Judah," said Naomi, as if she'd heard my thoughts.

"Eph-rah—" I repeated uncertainly, not knowing the word.

"Ephrathah is our town. Judah is our tribe." She glanced at her husband. "Israel is our people."

Orpah and I looked at each other. My friend's forehead was puckered up with worry.

"*Israelites!*" she hissed at me.

We knew a few things about Israelites. First, and most importantly, they worshipped different gods to us. To be exact, they worshipped only one god, and they claimed that none of the other gods were gods at all. It was hardly believable, but Orpah swore that it was true. A merchant at her mother's house had told her.

We also knew that the Israelites had fought against us Moabites. There had been disputes about the borders of our lands. I'd heard the old men in the village talk about it sometimes, when they sat at the edge of the fields at harvest time and gossiped. If only the Israelites had never come here out of the wilderness, they said, we'd all be living like kings.

So… did our village have room for a family of our old enemies? And worn-out-looking ones at that? Who possibly had diseases and probably had no money?

Maybe not.

Yet there was something about Naomi. I couldn't have said what it was exactly. I just knew that I wanted to know her.

So I said, "Yes, I'm sure there's room," and gestured towards the village.

Her cracked lips smiled. She took her husband's arm. "This is Elimelek, my husband," she told us proudly. "I am Naomi. And these—" She waved at the two boys, and they slunk forward. "These are my sons. Mahlon and Kilion."

Orpah let out an embarrassed giggle at being introduced to two older boys like that. I remained serious and important.

"It's this way," I said, turned around, and marched off.

We paced back towards home with them all straggling behind us. They went much slower than us— partly because of all their baggage, but also because we were young and strong, while they were exhausted from their long journey and their hunger. One of the boys didn't even have sandals on, just strips of cloth wrapped around his feet. No wonder he couldn't go very fast.

But I barely noticed that. I felt like some kind of war captain bringing spoils home from a battle. All thoughts of my mother, giving birth back at home, had been left far behind. This was *much* more interesting!

CHAPTER 3

A Rock from the Heavens

"Israelites?" Dinah demanded sharply, looking from me to Orpah to the poverty-stricken newcomers beside us. "Israelites?"

I opened my mouth to speak in the strangers' defence—then closed it again. Dinah was raising her eyebrows. She was scary when she raised her eyebrows.

"Well?" she asked.

"They…" I began, but fell silent. I glanced at the Israelite boys. They both had their gaze trained firmly on their feet.

Orpah was twisting her arms together behind her back as if that would somehow make her disappear.

Then Naomi pursed her lips. She adjusted the shawl that lay over her hair. She stepped forward.

"We just want to live," she said clearly, looking Dinah in the eyes. "We ask for shelter. We can work; we *want* to work. We're not cursed or diseased. We're not out-laws. We're just hungry."

Dinah folded her arms. "Why did you leave Israel?" she asked suspiciously.

"There's a famine," Naomi answered at once. "Not enough to eat. The harvest failed last year, and it'll fail again this year." She glanced at her husband. "Elimelek and I… we had no choice but to leave."

Dinah frowned. "Bad land, then."

"No!" cried Naomi angrily. "Our land isn't bad. It was given to us by God. It's been ours for generations. It's good land."

"But it has famine." Dinah shrugged. "Well, maybe you're just bad farmers, and that's why."

Naomi stayed silent at this. She pressed her lips together.

I thought maybe that meant her husband *was* a bad farmer, but she didn't want to say so.

"Do you have money?" asked Dinah abruptly. "Can you pay your way?"

"We can pay," Elimelek spoke up, managing not to cough as he nodded.

"Well, then, yes, you can sleep in my courtyard for a night or two. Two coins per night, how does that sound? And if your boys do some work for my husband…"

Dinah paused, looking the two boys up and down. I looked too. They both had short dark hair, slightly bulging eyes, and thin cheeks. Mahlon was about a head taller; he must be fourteen or so, I guessed. Nearly a grown man. His brother, Kilion, looked to be closer to us in age, but he had the same bony, hardened frame as his brother. They had different noses, though. Mahlon's was straight and narrow, like his father's. Kilion's was wider, like his mother's.

There were hardly any boys in our village. None at all that were a similar age to Orpah and me. I quite liked the thought of getting to know some.

Dinah was nodding. "If your boys do some work for my husband, and he approves of what they do, then maybe I'll let you stay longer. Maybe."

That was the best the Israelites were going to get.

Midday came, and there was no word from home. My two sisters, Reminah and Amam, had turned up in tears, saying they thought Ma was going to die—either that or the new baby would. It took me ages to calm them down, and as soon as I had, Bek decided that now was just the right time for *him* to become red in the face and start wailing about nothing at all.

I'd wanted to talk to the Israelite woman—to find out about Israel. What did it mean that their god had given them their land? And did they really worship only *one* god? And what were they going to do now that they were in Moab? But there had been no time.

At last, at last, my siblings lay snoozing quietly in the

shade. I took a few steps towards Naomi, framing my questions in my mind.

"Naomi…" I began.

"Ruth, come here!" called Dinah.

I stopped.

Orpah's mother was stirring a big pot of stew over the fire. "It's time to give the gods their offering," she said. "Come and say a prayer for your mother and the baby."

The family shrine stood in the centre of the wall at one end of the courtyard, opposite the house. It was a big slab of stone with a rectangular recess cut into the middle of it. In the recess stood the icons, together with a couple of oil lamps and the remains of a previous offering.

There were four of the little figures made of stone and wood. The great god Chemosh stood in the centre—his was the one that was carved with the most detail. Then there was the Lady by his side, made of cedarwood painted in bright colours. To the left was the ox-god, who, Dinah said, looked after our village and protected the fields. And on the right was the god of the household.

Dinah handed me a small clay dish, full of steaming stew. But as I stepped towards the shrine to give the gods their offering, I heard a mutter from one of the Israelite boys.

"There's one there that's just a rock," he said scornfully.

I stopped.

Dinah had heard it too. "*What* did you say?" she demanded.

It was the younger of the two boys who'd said it. Kilion. I could tell because a blush was spreading all the way across his snub nose and sunken cheeks. He looked scared, and didn't say anything.

"That *rock*," said Dinah angrily, "is a holy thing. It fell from the heavens. My husband's great-grandfather saw it. It comes from the gods."

Kilion still looked scared. But Naomi stood up to defend him.

"You can worship such gods if you want," she said crisply. "We don't."

She and Dinah stared at each other.

"Don't pretend you're something special," Dinah sneered. "Plenty of Israelites worship other gods. They make offerings just like everybody else. I've met the traders who sell them the statues."

"Well, those Israelites aren't *true* Israelites," Naomi replied stiffly. "*We* worship one God. The God who made the heavens and the earth. The God who gave us our land."

The two women stared at each other again.

I was worried. I was sure Dinah wouldn't want people like that under her roof—it was too risky. The gods might get angry.

She was going to kick the Israelites out. I could just feel it coming. But I wanted them to stay. They were *my* Israelites—I was the one who had found them and brought them here! And I had a lot of questions that I wanted the answers to!

I gazed from Naomi to Dinah and back again, barely noticing how tightly I was holding the clay dish in my hands.

Then, in the corner, Elimelek stood up shakily. "Wife," he said to Naomi, "we're not in Israel anymore."

He went up to the shrine and knelt down. "Please welcome us," he said to the idols on the lintel. And he kissed the stone.

There was a moment of silence. Elimelek coughed as he straightened up again and went back to his corner, not looking at his wife or sons.

Dinah smiled in satisfaction. "There we go. Not that hard." Then she looked at me. "Go on, Ruth. Make your offering."

Not meeting Naomi's gaze, I hurried forwards and knelt down in front of the shrine just as Elimelek had done. I placed the dish of stew in front of the gods.

"Great gods," I mumbled, "I give you this gift of food. In return, please keep my mother from harm, and her baby. May it be born healthy. May it live." I paused. "May it be a boy, to continue the family line."

I kissed the stone, just like always.

Then I sneaked a glance at Naomi. She was looking at me with a strange expression. It wasn't angry, or even disapproving. It was sad.

It was like she thought there was something I was missing out on.

CHAPTER 4

Harvest Time

A t last we had word from home: the labour was over and the baby had been born. My mother and the little one were both fine, but it was another girl. This made my father go tight-lipped and my mother moan at me that it was about time I left home to get married.

"Well, that is the way of things," said Dinah sagely when I complained about this in her presence. "Particularly in a family with as many mouths to feed as yours. You're very expensive, I'm afraid, Ruth."

I flushed. "I'm not just an expense. I do loads of work."

"Oh yes," she replied, "but you're destined to leave, aren't you? Your brother will always stay with your parents, but *you'll* soon belong somewhere else. So when your parents give you food and clothes, they're really providing for someone else's family."

I scowled.

"There's no point in complaining about the way the world works," said Dinah sharply. "Now go and do your chores. Your mother will be wondering where you are."

As I stomped away, she called after me in a softer voice. "Don't worry, though, Ruthy. You're too young yet for marriage. And your mother might not say it, but she needs you."

She certainly did. There was washing to do, and firewood to collect, and herbs to pick, and floors to sweep, and siblings to mind, and clothes to mend, and water to fetch, and grain to grind into flour. And over the next few weeks, it felt like *all* of it was done by *me*.

I barely had any time to spend with Orpah.

And I barely had any time to seek out Naomi.

I did see her two sons from time to time. To begin with they were just running errands for Dinah and her husband, but soon they started doing jobs for others in the village as well. Mahlon, the older one, still had no shoes, but it didn't seem to slow him down as he ran with a message here or heaved a jar of oil there. Kilion, the younger one, was less strong than his older brother, but still worked hard enough.

Their mother Naomi mostly stayed inside Dinah's courtyard. And Elimelek seemed to be too ill to do anything much.

But at harvest time, *everyone* came out to the fields.

There was a job for everyone during the barley harvest. The men swung their sickles, hefting them around and then around again to cut the barley at its base. The women pulled the cut stalks into big bundles, then stacked five or six bundles together to dry out. The children ran around behind them and picked up whatever bits the women had dropped. Everyone toiled, except the very oldest men sitting on their logs by the field-edges.

This was the first year that I counted as a woman and not a child, and I was not very happy about it. My hands were chafed red and cut in places, and my skin prickled with all the tiny bits of stalk and chaff that had stuck themselves through my clothes. What made it worse was that it wasn't fair. Orpah, over in her father's field, was still scampering around with the younger children. They'd put Kilion there to help with the women—he wasn't big enough yet to be much use with a sickle—and that meant Orpah wasn't needed.

I straightened up to look over into her field, which was the next plot to ours. There she was. She wasn't even picking up bits of grain; she was standing in the shade! Drinking water! And were those… were those raisins she was putting in her mouth? My stomach rumbled with jealousy.

"Is it time for a break?" I called to my mother. She had her arms around a bundle of barley and was pulling out a few stalks to twist together and tie it. She was grunting with the effort. She didn't even glance at me.

"I'm going to have a break," I shouted. Still no response.

"Right," I said, and ran off quickly in case she noticed and called me back.

By the time I reached the scrap of shade at the edge of Orpah's field, I was even hotter and redder in the face than before. I flopped down on the ground like a dead lizard.

"It's not fair," I said to Orpah. "I'm no bigger than you and I'm having to do a hundred times the work. And it's *boiling*."

"Have some raisins," she replied apologetically.

I reached out, still enjoying my horizontal position—then jumped as a voice coughed, close by. A male voice.

Mahlon.

"Would you like some water?" he asked pleasantly. His slightly protruding eyes were trying not to look at me, sprawled as I was in the dirt. My cheeks would have flushed with embarrassment if they hadn't been so red already.

I scrambled up to standing, pulling down my dress and catching my sweaty headscarf as it started to fall off my head.

"My mother just came back from the well with a fresh jar," Mahlon said quietly. He had it by his side. Orpah held out her waterskin and Mahlon took it from her, immersing it inside the jar so that it would fill up.

"Thank you," Orpah said shyly, and took back the

skin. "Would you… would you like some raisins?"

She had a whole cake of them—hundreds of the delicious dried fruits squished together in a circle as big as her palm. She broke off some and handed them to Mahlon. Then some to me. The three of us stood and munched awkwardly.

It was Mahlon who broke the silence.

"In Israel," he said thoughtfully in his strange accent, "the gleaning's done by poor people, not children."

"Gleaning?" I asked. That must be an Israelite word.

"You know, when they go around picking up the last few bits of grain that have been missed." He waved his hand towards the fields. "In Israel, we leave those bits. Then the poor can pick them up and take them for themselves."

I scoffed. I couldn't stop myself. "That's stupid," I said. "No wonder *you* didn't have enough to eat, if you were letting other people have some of it for free."

He flushed. "No… That's not…"

"Anyway," I interrupted, "there aren't any poor people here. Are there?" I appealed to Orpah.

She looked doubtful. "Well," she said, "there's Zowelah…"

"The widow?" asked Mahlon interestedly. "The one with the cracks in her wall?"

"Zowelah isn't poor," I insisted.

Zowelah *was* poor, though. It was hard being a widow. Her only daughter had left to get married years ago.

Zowelah had had a son too, but he'd died as a baby. And her husband had died at around the same time. Zowelah had been on her own for as long as I'd been alive—and before then, too.

She was all right, though, I thought. She seemed to survive, didn't she, just like everybody else?

I'd never really thought about it before.

"Is she here?" Mahlon asked, looking around. "My mother was asking after her. She visits her sometimes. She said she's lonely."

I bit my lip. Zowelah did normally make it out for the harvest. But this time she wasn't here.

"I'm sure she's fine," I answered coldly.

There was silence.

"Why *do* people leave the grain like you said?" Orpah asked. "In the fields in Israel? Don't they need it?"

Mahlon frowned in thought. "Well, yes… but then, so do the poor. They…" He hesitated, then plunged on. "Well, poor Israelites are still Israelites. Children of Abraham. Part of God's people. And God is kind to us all."

I put my last raisin in my mouth and chewed it, feeling uncomfortable.

I didn't understand this Israelite god. How could you worship only one? And how could he be *kind*? Gods showed favour to you if you gave them the right offerings, in theory. But really they did what they wanted. So… what did it mean for a god to be kind and loyal? I didn't get it.

Mahlon gave a slow smile. "Well," he said, hefting his water jar, "I'd better get along and see if anyone else wants—"

His voice trailed off.

"What?" I cried, whirling round to see where his gaze had gone to. "What is it?"

But the field was such a confusion of people and the sun was so bright, I couldn't spot what he was looking at.

I heard it instead.

A huge, ragged scream.

A guttering of horrible sobs.

And, finally, I saw that it was all coming from Naomi.

CHAPTER 5

He Just Collapsed

Naomi knelt over Elimelek, moaning. She slapped his cheeks, then balled her fists and hit him in the chest—but nothing was going to make him respond, we could all see that. He just lay there, limp. Lifeless. Dead.

Kilion stood just behind Naomi, his face pale. "He just—he just collapsed," he was muttering mindlessly. "How is he—how do you—"

Mahlon, ignoring him, went forward and pulled his mother upright, squeezing her into an embrace.

The whole village had gathered around them—Orpah and I included. We stayed back, though, while the adults crowded in front of us. Naomi was still moaning; it was a deep animal sound, a horrible sound. But there were other voices too now. Dinah was saying something about the gods. My father was talking about moving the body.

I felt like half of me was slipping sideways. I didn't even really know Elimelek, but he'd been alive and now he was dead. Just like that.

I took a step backwards.

Then I said, "We should go and check on Zowelah."

Orpah looked frightened. "Are you sure?"

"We should go and check on her," I said firmly. "She's lonely. Come on."

⁖⟩⟩⟩⟩—

The door on Zowelah's house was just a few uneven planks nailed together with gaps in between. It leaned against the opening, doing a bad job of blocking out draughts. There was no hesitating now—I grabbed it and shoved it aside, calling Zowelah's name as I did so, and peering into the dark doorway.

There was no answer.

"Zowelah!" I called again, taking a step forward so that Orpah wouldn't see how scared I was. "Maybe she's asleep," I said confidently.

"I don't—" Orpah began, but I interrupted her by calling out the widow's name again.

"Zowelah! Hello?"

My eyes were adjusting to the gloom now. I was entering one of two small rooms. This one was even smaller than I remembered it from the last time I came in here, when I was little. Dirtier as well. Though, someone had clearly made an effort recently. A space in the middle of the floor had been swept and there was a pile of cooking pans that looked freshly scrubbed.

I wrinkled my nose. I'd never really thought about how grim life must be for Zowelah, living alone. Grim and dirty. She barely had the strength to potter down to the fields; she certainly couldn't wash clothes or sweep floors. Or scrub pans.

So who had done these?

Orpah was in the room too by now. She touched the wall—there were cracks on the inside, just like on the outside. "How can she bear to live here?" she whispered.

"She has no choice," I replied, swallowing. "This is why everyone wants sons, who'll be around when they're old. To avoid this."

Opposite the entrance was another doorway, this one concealed by a curtain. Zowelah must be through there. Sleeping, probably.

Probably.

"What if—" said Orpah, but she didn't dare to finish her sentence.

"Look," I said in a voice that was a bit too loud. I used my foot to nudge a basket I'd spotted on the floor. "Someone must have brought this. A package of food?"

Orpah bent to look. "Yes. Oh!" She reached into the basket and pulled out a little clay bowl with a few dried olives in it. "This is ours. My mother's. Naomi asked to borrow it. I'm sure it's the same one."

Our eyes met.

"Then… Naomi has been bringing Zowelah food," I said. "Even though she has so little herself."

"And she must be the one who scrubbed those pans," added Orpah.

There was silence. Then we both turned again to the ragged curtain hanging in the doorway to the next room.

Orpah reached out and grabbed my hand. Taking a deep breath, we went through the curtain together.

Zowelah was asleep when we found her—but she wasn't well. There was a grating sound deep in her chest, and when she woke up she was too stiff to move. We tried to do a few things for her—tidying and so on—but we knew there wasn't much point anymore. She wasn't going to get out of bed again.

A few days after Elimelek died, Zowelah died too.

After that, I decided that I wanted to be like Naomi: I wanted to be kind. I found ways to visit Dinah's house and help the Israelite woman. I went to the well for her, even though I hated having to carry the heavy water jars all the way back. I patched up an old pair of my father's shoes and presented them to Mahlon. I spoke in a low voice because I knew Naomi was grieving and shouldn't be disturbed too much. I even helped clear out

Zowelah's house, and didn't complain about having to be part of the funeral.

A few weeks after the two deaths, I came out of our house to see Mahlon inspecting the cracks in the walls of Zowelah's home. Naomi stood beside her son, her arms folded.

"You see, I don't think it'll be that hard to repair," Mahlon was saying. "Ma? I asked some of the men, and they said—"

"I don't care," snapped Naomi.

"But Ma," Mahlon reasoned, "don't you want to have your own home again? It's a good plan, I promise you. Nobody else has claimed this house yet. And once we've moved in, no one will stop us—"

"No," Naomi said curtly. She pursed her lips. "This isn't our home. We're not going to stay here."

"But we can't go back, not while there's still famine."

"We're *Israelites*, Mahlon," Naomi said. "Israelites. Not Moabites."

"But we're in Moab for now, Ma!" Mahlon insisted.

I stayed motionless. Neither of them had spotted me yet.

"We're descended from Abraham," Naomi said to her son.

"Ma, I know this—"

"We're descended from *Abraham*," she said again in a warning tone. "And Abraham was called into our land by God, *personally*. The Lord appeared to him, and told him he would make his name great, and make his family into a great nation. He told him he'd give his descendants the land. The land of *Israel*, Mahlon, not the land of Moab.

"Abraham and his wife Sarah couldn't have children," she went on, "and they wondered what the future would be. But finally our great God did give them a son, Isaac. And Isaac had a son, Jacob. And the Lord said to him, too, *I will make a nation of you, I will give you a land, and I will be your God.* So you see, the three things go together: people, land, God."

"I know," Mahlon said wearily.

Naomi pursed her lips again, this time with pride. "We are children of Abraham, Isaac, and Jacob. We are Israelites, of the tribe of Judah. What are you thinking, Mahlon? Are you going to forget who you are? Are you going to, I don't know, marry a Moabite girl and *settle down* here? No, you are not! You're an *Israelite!* You belong with God's people!"

"I understand that, Ma," answered Mahlon patiently. "I'm not suggesting we stay here for ever. I'm just saying, this house is empty and we could move into it. Just for a bit. Until we're ready to go back." He turned to the walls again. "I really think we could repair this. And the old lady liked you, didn't she? Wouldn't she have been pleased to think that you were going to move into her house, instead of all these Moabites who never bothered to look after her?"

I bit my lip.

"Let me at least *try* to repair it," said Mahlon.

There was silence.

I could see that Mahlon was going to take that as a yes.

CHAPTER 6

The Israelites Next Door

Mahlon's plan worked. The Israelites did move into Zowelah's house. They had to rebuild the whole wall, but they moved in.

Now that they were only next door, it was easy to get to know them. My father would often call on the boys to help him with something (grumbling that he wished he had grown-up sons of his own to help instead). And I would find any excuse to go and sit with Naomi. Orpah came too sometimes.

Even though Naomi had spoken so strongly against staying in Moab, she didn't seem to mind us spending time with her. In fact, I thought she liked it. My tactic was to ask questions about the history of her people and about the Israelite God—since that was what she was so proud of. And she was always happy to tell us a story. Sometimes it would be about Abraham, the ancestor of all the Israelites, or his grandson Jacob. Sometimes it would be about when the Israelites were slaves in Egypt and God rescued them. Sometimes it would be about the women of Israel. After a few months, Orpah and I knew the stories well enough to start having arguments about which was the best.

The following spring, news came from Israel: the harvest looked bad once again. The Israelites would have to stay.

My mother looked pleased. "Perhaps they'll stay for ever. I didn't like the idea of having Israelites here at first, but the boys are a good addition to the village."

"I wouldn't mind having a son-in-law like one of those boys," my father said.

My mother looked at me pointedly.

"Ma, no," I said. "No. I see what you're thinking. But Naomi will never let one of her sons marry me. They won't marry anyone who isn't an Israelite. And also, they don't want to stay in Moab. They believe that God—I mean, their god—gave them their land. He promised it to Abraham, their ancestor. It's the only place where they can worship God—*their* god— properly."

"Well, why did they come to Moab, then?" asked my father dismissively.

"It does *look* like they're going to stay, Ruth," said my mother. "Particularly if the famine lasts. And your father is right. Mahlon would be a good husband for you."

"Naomi will say no if you ask her," I answered.

But to my complete surprise, when they *did* ask her, she said yes.

She frowned, but she said yes.

～～～～～

We didn't get married straight away. Mahlon wanted to make the old widow's house a bit bigger first, particularly as Kilion would also get married before long. And I had a lot of weaving to do before we could have a wedding.

But at the start of my sixteenth summer, we married, and I moved in with the Israelites.

I immediately began a campaign to get Orpah to marry Kilion, and it was successful; she moved in a year later.

But… the next bit of the story is going to be hard for me to talk about, I'm sorry.

We lived together for six years. They weren't perfect years, of course. Neither Orpah nor I had a child—not even a daughter—and that was, honestly, a worry. But we were still young, and Naomi always told us that we had to wait until the Lord God was ready to give us a child.

"He's loyal to our people," she said.

But then…

Hmm. I told you it would be hard for me to talk about.

Then, the worst thing I could ever have imagined happened.

Mahlon got sick. And so did Kilion.

Really, really sick.

On Mahlon's final day of life, there were a few moments when the fever seemed to fade away and he was himself again. He was weak, and still trembling, but he was Mahlon.

He reached out and took my hand. "I'm sorry, Ruth. I… I'm sorry."

I swallowed hard. "Don't be sorry. We've been all right, haven't we? I'll be all right."

"Kilion will look after you," he said urgently. "Or you can… or you can marry someone else…"

"No," I answered, squeezing his hand. "I won't abandon this family."

"You're so kind…" Mahlon whispered. "If only we had another brother… You could marry him… Then you'd be safe."

"I'll be fine," I told him.

"Kilion. Kilion will look after you," he said.

I did not have the heart to tell him that Kilion was lying sick with the same fever, just on the other side of the wall.

I squeezed his hand again, harder. This time it wasn't

to comfort him, it was to comfort me. Or, to make me feel like I had something to hold on to.

But Mahlon didn't seem to notice. His eyes had closed and his hand had gone limp again.

"I don't want to be a widow," I said in a tiny voice.

I let go of Mahlon and pressed my hands against my eyes, trying to hold back the thick tears. But I couldn't stop them.

"Is it a curse?" I asked my husband miserably. "Is the God of Israel angry with you for marrying me, when you should have married an Israelite? And angry with Kilion as well? You've always said he's a kind god, but is that not true? Is it all our fault?"

Mahlon did not reply.

"I wish I'd been born an Israelite," I said. "I wish… I wish…" But my words dissolved into tears.

Then Naomi was there, her hand touching my hair. I reached out for her mindlessly. "I don't want him to die," I sobbed into her chest. "I don't want him to die!"

Naomi tucked my head under her chin and rocked me like a baby. "I know, my daughter," she said.

We stayed like that, watching over Mahlon, for a long while.

He died that day, and Kilion died a few days later. Our poor mother-in-law had now lost her husband and both her sons. Orpah and I wept and wept and wept, but Naomi was inconsolable. She barely ate for a week. Naomi had never been fat, but now she was worryingly wispy.

We buried her boys beside Elimelek—a little way outside the village, since they'd never fully belonged there.

It was not long afterwards that another traveller arrived—one who'd been through Israel. He told us that everything was fine there now. The famine was over. People were getting on with their lives.

I saw the look in Naomi's eyes as she heard those words. That bittersweet glint, mixing sadness with hope. I knew at once what was coming.

She stood up, pursing her lips, and drew her shawl across her thin shoulders. She looked at Orpah, and then she looked at me.

"I want to go home," she said.

CHAPTER 7

Beyond the Boundary Stone

We set out at dawn. All three of us had a bag heavy with food and clothes and cooking gear, but we'd sold everything else. Old Zowelah's house was empty again, ready for some family or other to get too big and need a second home to move into. My uncle and aunt, perhaps—they had a two-year-old now, and another baby on the way. But then, my sister Amam would marry soon and provide more space in my parents' house.

There's room for you to go back there if you want, a voice in my head said. *You don't have to leave with Naomi.*

But I shook my head. I'd made my decision.

I looked around. The barley on either side of the path was almost knee-high, and orangey-green in the early sunlight. And there was the old boundary stone that marked the very edge of our village. Someone had left a grain-cake on it as an offering to the gods. I smiled.

It did look like a strange hat, perched on the head of a man wearing a lichen-covered cloak.

Beside me, Orpah whimpered.

"The old marker," she hissed. "My ma always said… she always said I shouldn't go further than this. When I was little."

"I know," I said.

"She said if I went further than this, I would be outside the protection of the village gods."

Orpah had stopped walking. She placed her hand on the grey stone. She looked at me with scared eyes.

"Well," I said breezily, "now we'll be under the protection of Naomi's god. The God of Israel. He's powerful everywhere—you know Naomi always says that. Just think about all the stories she's told us. He's kind. He's loyal to his people."

"Are we his people?" Orpah whispered.

I hesitated. "Well, we are sort of, aren't we? Even if we're not…" I trailed off. Then I tried again. "Anyway, Naomi definitely is. And we're with her."

We looked along the path, where Naomi was still plodding onwards. Her back was bent under her load. We'd made sure she had the least to carry, but even so, she was having to work very hard. She had so little strength.

"Come *on*," I told Orpah. "We can't change our minds now."

But Naomi could.

As I pulled Orpah along towards her, Naomi stopped and wheeled back around to face us. Her face was screwed up like a baby's—in anger? In sorrow? I couldn't tell.

"Go back," she cried, flapping her hands at us. "Go back, both of you, to your mothers' homes!"

"Naomi," I started to say firmly, but her wild eyes silenced me.

"Go back!" She was weeping. "May the Lord show you kindness, but go back."

Orpah dumped her load on the ground and stepped towards our mother-in-law.

I did the same. "Naomi…" I tried again. But she beat my words away with her hands.

"You've shown kindness," she sobbed, "to your… to your dead hu-husbands! And to me! But go back! May the Lord g-grant that each of you will find rest in the home of, of another husband."

She reached out with trembling hands, and grasped Orpah's face, kissing her on the forehead. Then she did the same to me. "Goodbye, goodbye. You shouldn't come with me."

But I cried, "No!"

I seized Naomi's hand as she tried to pull it away. "*Not* goodbye! We're going back with you to your people." I glanced at Orpah. "We're your family. We want to come."

Naomi shook her head miserably. "No. Go back home. Why would you come with me?"

"Because…" I began, but I couldn't put it into words.
Because I care about you?
Because I wish I could be part of your people?
Because I want to see if I could be loved by your God?
It would all sound stupid if I said it out loud.

Really, Naomi was right. I'd been over the arguments a thousand times with Orpah already. Technically we belonged with Naomi, but now that our husbands were dead, what did that even mean? We were free to marry again, but who'd marry us in Israel? We were foreigners, outsiders. Naomi's family might just refuse to have anything to do with us, and then where would we be?

But Naomi needed us. She really did. And that had to count for something.

Naomi had smelled my hesitation. "Am I going to have any more sons," she asked wildly, "who could become your husbands? No! I'm too old." She sniffed. "Even if I thought there was still hope for me… even if I had a husband tonight and then gave birth to sons… would you wait until they grew up? Would you stay unmarried for them? No!"

She tore her hand away from me and staggered backwards. "This is more bitter for me than for you," she spat, suddenly angry. Her voice had gone low and dark. "The Lord's hand has turned against me."

It felt like an age that we stood there, the three of us, with Orpah and me each making the decision of our lives while Naomi sobbed in front of us.

Would we go with her, and leave everything else we knew?

Or would we go back to our own village?

And was it true that God had turned against Naomi? Would we be cursed if we went with her?

I noticed that Orpah was crying—not loudly like Naomi but silently, with tears running down her face. She clasped Naomi's hands again, but gently, and then released them.

"Goodbye," she whispered to her, and then looked at me, waiting for me to do the same.

"No," I said. "No."

But my friend shook her head slowly, turned, and walked away.

"Look," said Naomi, sounding calmer now. "Your sister-in-law is going back to her people and her gods. Go back with her. Go home."

She pursed her lips, looking determined.

I pursed mine too.

"*Don't* urge me to leave you," I said. "Don't urge me to turn back from you." I put my hands on her bony shoulders and gripped them firmly. "Where you go, I will go. Where you stay, I will stay. Your people will be my people. Your God will be my God."

Naomi's eyes widened.

"Where you die," I added, "*I* will die. And that's where I'll be buried." I was spitting out my words now. "May the Lord deal with me severely if even *death* separates you and me!"

My fingernails were digging into the fabric of Naomi's dress. I loosened them, and kissed her head just like she'd kissed mine. I brushed the tears away from her withered cheeks.

Then I picked up my bag, and Orpah's too, and pulled their straps across my chest.

"Let's go to Israel," I said.

CHAPTER 8

I Tell a Story

The further we got from Moab, the less Naomi talked. So I talked instead. I repeated to her all the stories she'd told me—about Abraham, about Isaac, about Jacob, and about how her people had first come to their land. I could tell she was listening because after a few stories she started correcting me on details I'd got wrong. After a few stories more, I started deliberately getting things wrong—that way she'd *have* to talk.

"Let me tell you the story of the grandsons of Abraham," I said cheerily one morning as we started the day's trek. "They were called Jacob and Eshob."

"Esau," Naomi said irritably.

"Oh yes, sorry," I answered, "Jacob and Esau. They were twins, but they were very different to one another. Jacob was smooth-skinned and liked staying at home. Esau was very hairy, and he liked to dance."

"Hunt." Naomi ground her teeth. "He liked to hunt."

"Oh yes," I said again, "of course, he liked to hunt."

"Maybe you'd better not tell this story," Naomi said in a stony voice, "since you keep getting it wrong."

"Well, would *you* like to tell it instead?" I answered politely.

She gave no answer.

I sighed. "All right. I promise I'll get it right from now on. I'll tell you… I'll tell you the story of Jacob and his wives."

She still said nothing. I decided this meant she consented.

I took a deep breath. This story had to cheer Naomi up. I had to tell it in just the right way.

"Esau…" I began, then stopped myself at once. Esau took a wife who was not an Israelite, and it didn't go very well. There was no way I wanted to remind Naomi of *that*.

"What I meant to say," I went on, "was that *Jacob* had grown old enough to get married. And he decided to travel far from home to find a wife."

Naomi pursed her lips.

I went on hurriedly. "He travelled north, out of the land which God had promised to his grandfather Abraham and their family. He travelled and travelled and travelled. He reached the place where Abraham had been born. And there he met…" I spread out my hands dramatically and softened my voice. "Rachel! A relative of his. She had come out of the town to bring her sheep to drink at the well. She was beautiful and dutiful, and she was the very person Jacob had hoped to meet. So he jumped forward and rolled away the heavy stone that guarded the well, so that her flocks could drink. Then Rachel took Jacob to meet her father.

"Jacob agreed to work for seven years in return for Rachel's hand in marriage. Seven whole years! But they seemed like only a few days to Jacob because of his love for Rachel. Yet Rachel's father, Laban, had a trick up his sleeve. When the seven years were over, he didn't give Rachel in marriage to Jacob as he had promised. He gave him... *Leah*.

"Leah was Rachel's older sister. She was much less beautiful, but she was the oldest, and so Laban wanted her to get married first. She had a veil on so Jacob couldn't see that it was her and not his beloved Rachel. By the time Jacob realised, it was too late! Leah was his wife.

"Of course, Jacob protested. *Why have you deceived me?* he cried to Leah's father. But Laban just shrugged. He told him he had to marry the older daughter first, but he could have the younger one too—if he worked for Laban for another seven years.

"Seven whole years! But Jacob agreed at once. Anything if he could get to marry Rachel. So he kept on working for Laban—without any wages. But despite that, he grew rich, because the Lord God is kind and loyal to the family of Abraham.

"The Lord God was kind to Leah, as well. He gave her four sons: Reuben, Simeon, Levi and Judah. And each of these became the father of one of the tribes of Israel! In fact, God gave Jacob twelve sons in all. As well as Reuben, Simeon, Levi, and Judah, there were Dan, Naphtali, Gad…" I was quite proud that I knew all the names.

But Naomi interrupted my flow. "If only you and Orpah had been more like Rachel and Leah," she said sadly.

I reddened. "How do you mean?"

I expected her to say that we weren't really Israelites. But instead she said mournfully, "If only you'd had children."

I opened my mouth. Then I closed it again. What could I say?

"Or, or… if only *I'd* had another son," she continued. "Then he could have married one of you after his poor brothers died. You could have raised up children for Mahlon."

"What? What do you mean?"

"There's a custom in Israel. If a man and his wife have no children, and the man dies, the man's brother is supposed to marry the widow. Then there can be children. The family line continues. And the firstborn son of the new marriage is counted as the son of the wife's original husband."

I tried to understand what Naomi had just said. "So… if you'd had another son… I would have married him after Mahlon died."

"Yes."

"And if we'd had a child, then… that child would have been seen as Mahlon's?"

I must have been pulling a confused face, because Naomi said sourly, "It's a good custom. Apart from any-thing else, it would have meant you were looked after properly in the house of a husband, with a child to look after you in your old age. Instead of which, here you are with me in the middle of nowhere. Even worse off than that poor old woman who used to live in our house."

I bit my lip. "I don't think that's true—" I began.

"But I have no more sons," she interrupted with a moan. "And it's too late for me to have any more. And it's too late for you too now, because you insisted on coming with me instead of going home like you should have done." She gave a dramatic sigh. "So we're all alone."

We trudged a few more paces in silence.

Then I gritted my teeth. I would *not* have this. I was supposed to be cheering her up!

"The Lord is kind," I said, "isn't he? He's kind, and he's loyal to his people. So we're not all alone. We're going to Judah, where your family has always lived, and we're going to be fine. Even if—even if there aren't any more children. Or any more husbands."

There was silence for a moment. Only the sound of our footsteps in the dust. Then Naomi said, "Do you know what happened to Rachel in the end? The beloved wife of Jacob?"

I said, "No."

"She died on the road to Ephrathah." Naomi looked at me mournfully. "That's where *we're* going."

CHAPTER 9

The House of Bread

Ephrathah. Also known as Bethlehem, which means the house of bread. Not a good name for a place where there was a famine.

But there certainly wasn't a famine anymore.

The barley was already ripe—we could see the fields even at some distance from the town, and they were a delicious, beautiful golden brown. There were patches of green wheat as well, and we passed a grove of gnarly fig trees starting to blossom. A boy was sitting underneath one of them, watching the road. His hand rested on a thick club: he must be there to guard the trees, ready for when they produced fruit. He glared at us as we went past. Naomi glared back.

Now that we were getting closer, it was all I could do to keep plodding on beside my mother-in-law and not run ahead. I could swear she was going slower than usual. Shuffling along as if she didn't want to get there.

But this was her *home*! We were there at last! We would be safe in a town instead of risking our lives sleeping in strange places along the road!

I caught Naomi's hand and squeezed it, trying to pull her forward a little and communicate some of my excitement. But still she kept on shuffling. At least she was going forwards.

I turned my attention to what I could see up ahead. We were going to pass another patch of trees, this time almonds. The nuts would be nowhere near ready to harvest yet, but to my surprise there was another savage-looking boy leaning against one of the trunks with his arms folded. What was the point in guarding trees with no food on them? I started to feel uneasy. I'd thought the Israelites were supposed to be generous with their crops, not overprotective of them.

I looked further ahead to where the path reached the town. A long wall ran all around it in a circle. On one side of the wall, the hillside rose steeply. On the other side it dropped down—then rose again to make more hills, then more. It made me feel a little bit sick to look at all those slopes. I wasn't sure I'd ever be able to get used to country like this.

But I clenched my hands around the strap of my bags and told myself not to worry. This was my new home. We were going to find Naomi's family, and they'd be so pleased to have her back, and hopefully they'd welcome me too. Hopefully.

We were getting to the gate. Just outside it was... an unmistakable shape. A flattish stone with an alcove carved into it and flowers placed on top.

I squinted. Yes, I was right in what I had seen. It was a shrine! A shrine, just like the one at Dinah's house.

"I thought Israelites didn't worship god-statues like that," I said to Naomi. "I thought you didn't have shrines."

Her mouth was a line. "We don't. We shouldn't."

Then she pointed. "Look. It's half-destroyed."

She was right. Now that we were closer, we could see that the flowers were long dead. Half the petals had blown away. The stone was blackened around the bottom where a fire had been set around it, and someone had taken a chisel and hacked a big chunk off the top. The alcove for the statues was empty. The shrine was dead. Destroyed.

Still, it had been in use once, and I knew that wasn't what the God of Israel had told his people to do.

But Naomi's attention was no longer on the battered shrine. She was staring at the open gates of the town with an unreadable expression on her face.

"Ephrathah," she said. "Bethlehem."

We'd arrived.

"It was him. *He* took my goat. I know it was him. He's hated me ever since we were children. My own brother, stealing from underneath my nose!"

The woman had a red face, a striped headdress and one hand on her hip. The other hand was clutching the wrist of a worried-looking man who stood beside her.

"I didn't take her. I didn't," he said.

"What have you done with her, hey? What have you done with my pride and joy?"

"I've done nothing. I don't know where your goat is!"

"Don't lie to me! How can you lie before the elders of the town? Do you have no shame?"

This was what we'd walked into.

We'd barely taken ten steps beyond the gate. There was an acacia tree planted just inside the walls, shading a patch of flat ground on which a few stumps had been placed as seats. Five or six grey-haired men sat on the stumps, and the woman was gesticulating in their direction.

"I know he did it," she shouted, then glared at her brother again. "You've taken her off and sold her somewhere. Then used the money to buy all that fancy cloth for your wife so that she can parade around like a great big ostrich. How else do you explain that, huh? How else could you afford such a thing?"

"Woman." One of the grey-haired men stood up and made a calming gesture. "Peace. Let's talk this over properly. What is your accusation?"

"What's my accusation? My brother, my own flesh-and-blood, good-for-nothing brother, has stolen my goat!"

"I didn't," maintained the worried-looking man.

"He did, and I'll tell you the proof. He—"

"Peace!" said the older man again, but in a more dangerous voice this time. "This is not the way to solve a dispute. Do you have no respect for the elders of your town? Sit, and we will hear both sides."

Reluctantly, the red-faced woman allowed herself to be led towards another wide stone that lay beside the others. She sat at one end of it, and her brother perched at the other end. The grey-haired man returned to his own seat, and started to ask them questions.

The other elders leaned towards the woman and her brother too—except one. A man with a thin face and an embroidered hat. He was looking at *us*. First at Naomi, then at me. He wasn't staring exactly, just taking us in with interest and curiosity. But it didn't seem friendly.

I looked away, blushing. When I looked up again, the man's attention had turned to the red-faced woman and her brother.

"Can we go?" I whispered to Naomi, wanting to get away.

She heaved a sigh, and led me deeper into Bethlehem.

CHAPTER 10

Talk of the Town

But where were we going? We hadn't really discussed a plan for what we'd do once we actually reached Bethlehem. I'd just assumed that Naomi would take us to the house of her closest relatives—to Elimelek's family. They would be the ones who ought to take responsibility for Naomi and look after her. If these Ephrathites actually obeyed their God, that was.

It was my turn to go slowly. I hugged my bundle close to my chest, feeling my heart thumping inside my ribcage. I was scared suddenly. What if they didn't accept us? What if they didn't look after us? What if they threw me out and said I was just a dirty Moabite and could never be part of God's people?

The houses of Bethlehem were closer together than in our village at home, and there were more of them. Naomi led me around the corner of one. I glimpsed a little garden behind a wall, with beanstalks and leafy herbs growing in it. The next house along was not a house at all but a potter's workshop; there was a roof but no walls, and underneath the roof a man was treading clay in a big vat. He stared at us. "Is that...? I can't believe it... is that *Naomi*?"

But Naomi hurried on.

We turned another corner. And another. Here there was a wider street, filled with people. Naomi immediately flinched and darted around a corner again, leaving me rushing to keep up.

But we'd been spotted.

"Naomi!" A loud voice came from behind us. "I thought it was you. Naomi!"

I turned around to see a woman of about Naomi's age, rushing up behind us. "Naomi!" she called. "Stop!"

Naomi stopped. Then slowly, she turned around.

"Naomi," said the woman breathlessly. "I can't believe it. You're back." She looked behind her, where another woman was following. "Melchi! I said it was her, didn't I? I told you!"

Melchi came to a halt and stood there with her hands on her hips, looking amazed. "You did, Joanna."

The first woman turned back to Naomi. "We all thought you were dead. I never thought I'd ever see you again."

The potter from a few streets ago had extracted himself from the vat of clay and was hopping towards us as well, still cleaning his legs with a rag. "This will be the talk of the town!" he cried excitedly. "The talk of the town!"

"Melchi, go and find everyone else," commanded Joanna. "They're not going to believe it. Can this really be Naomi?"

"Did someone say Naomi?" came another woman's voice, this one from a window above our heads. "Naomi the wife of Elimelek? They've come back?"

At the mention of her husband's name, Naomi started to shrink into herself. I swallowed.

"Naomi, where is he?" said Joanna. "Where's your husband? Where are your boys?" She paused, noticing me for the first time. "Who's this girl?"

Naomi's eyebrows furrowed dark over her eyes. Her lips were pressed together so that all the wrinkles around them showed. She said nothing.

"Sweetheart…" said the woman in the window above us.

Then Naomi's mouth burst apart suddenly. "Don't call me *sweet*," she snarled. "Call me *bitter*. The Almighty has made my life very bitter. The Lord has brought misfortune on me."

And she burst into tears.

I'd seen Naomi cry before, but never quite this much. It was as if some damp clothes, left out on a rock to dry, had been caught in a sudden flood. Her face was all crumpled up and her voice was thick with grief.

"I went away full," she sobbed, "but the Lord has

brought me back empty."

But Joanna, the woman in the street, wasn't crying. "Melchi," she called loudly to her friend, "go and tell everyone. Tell them Naomi is back. Her husband is dead. Her sons are dead." She narrowed her eyes. "Looks like it wasn't such a good idea to go off to Moab after all, huh?"

After that, Naomi refused to speak.

The Ephrathite women wandered off to share the gossip. The potter went back to his clay, shaking his head sadly. Naomi sank down against a wall, clutched her baggage in her bony hands, and closed her eyes. And no matter what I tried, I could not get her to open them and talk to me.

"We just have to find your relatives," I said. "Just think, soon you'll be being welcomed home."

Nothing.

"Come on, they can't be far away," I tried. "Just a few steps more."

Nothing. She didn't move one muscle. She just sat there.

"Naomi, we've got to do *something*," I said.

Still nothing.

"I'm hungry," I wheedled.

No reply.

With a growl of frustration, I dumped my bundle next to my mother-in-law's huddled form and stamped my foot. "NAOMI."

She ignored me.

"Right," I said. "I am going to find some food. When I get back, perhaps you can bring yourself to talk to me. Since I have done absolutely nothing wrong. Since all I have done for the last *two months* and more is to look after you, be kind to you, try to cheer you up, cook you food, fetch you water, and generally be the best daughter-in-law I know how to be."

I hovered there for a moment, waiting to see if my speech had had any effect.

One eyelid flickered in Naomi's wrinkled face.

That was it.

I stamped my foot again, twisted round, and marched off.

CHAPTER 11

Nobody Wants a Moabite

I went away full, but the Lord has brought me back empty. Those had been her words. "Thanks, Naomi," I muttered bitterly as I stomped along through the unfamiliar town.

It had been a mistake to come here. Naomi didn't love me—she'd just put up with me while her sons were alive. She didn't want me. She'd even told me to stay in Moab, hadn't she? Why hadn't I listened? I wished I'd listened. I could be back there with Orpah right now. I'd be eating something tasty, and my feet wouldn't be sore from days of travelling, and we'd be full of laughter because we'd be where we belonged.

Instead of which I was here, in stupid Bethlehem Ephrathah, surrounded by stupid Israelites, with a stupid mother-in-law who wasn't even grateful, and a god who possibly hated us.

I screwed up my face, trying not to cry. I knew I was

thinking things that I didn't really mean. I knew Naomi
did love me. I just... I felt overwhelmed.

I turned a corner and slowed down as I saw that I was
entering the busier part of town again, an open space
bustling with people and animals. Suddenly I felt very
exposed. A young woman shouldn't be out on her own
in a strange town. Especially not a young *foreign* woman.
I drew my headscarf forward so that it veiled my face a
little. I wished my husband were still alive and by my side.

But wishing was not going to do me any good. I
forced myself forward. What I needed was food: I really
was hungry. I was sure Naomi must be as well. We just
needed something to eat and then everything would feel
all right again, and we could get back to finding Naomi's
relatives and sorting things out.

Then my nostrils caught a smell.

Marjoram. My favourite herb. It smelled round and
warm and tasty. I could hear a sizzle of oil, and the soft
bubbling of thick liquid. My stomach felt like a deep,
empty chasm all of a sudden as I looked around trying
to locate the person who was cooking.

Over there. An old man sat in a shady nook between
two houses. He'd dug a little ditch in the ground and lit
a fire in it, over which he'd put a big cooking pot. He
had a pile of flat loaves next to him—too many for him
to eat on his own. He must be selling them.

My stomach rumbled hopefully.

The man was half-veiled by the delicious-smelling

steam from his pot, but he batted it away with one hand as I came closer. I saw that one eye was milky with blindness, but the other scrutinised me carefully.

"Do you have money?" he snapped.

"Yes," I replied nervously, fumbling with the pouch that I'd hidden in my belt. "Can I buy bread? Two loaves?"

He named his price. I gulped. I did have enough, but our little store of coins would soon run out if we had to keep buying food at that kind of cost.

I handed him his coins, and he grabbed two of his loaves and slung them over to me across the fire. I only just managed to catch them.

"They could have gone in the flames!" I cried angrily. "Or the dirt!"

The man shrugged. "Your problem, not mine, Moabite girl."

Then a new voice came from behind me.

"You! The Moabite girl!"

Was it so obvious that I was foreign? I turned around slowly, fearfully... and saw Melchi, one of the women who'd accosted Naomi before. She was a thin woman with a face that looked like it loved to interfere. She was jabbing her finger at me.

"You. What's your name?"

"Ruth," I told her softly, making a little curtsey.

"You've come back with Naomi from Moab," she stated.

"Yes."

"Hmm." She narrowed her eyes. "So what are you? Her servant? She doesn't look rich enough to have a servant."

"I'm her daughter-in-law," I said, trying to sound proud of it.

"Her daughter-in-law?!" Melchi's eyebrows shot up. "You married her son?"

"That *is* what daughter-in-law generally means," I said.

Melchi clicked her tongue. "None of your disrespect, Moabite girl. You should consider where you are."

"I'm in Ephrathah," I replied evenly. "Ephrathah, also known as Bethlehem, in the territory of Judah, in the land of Israel. Judah is your tribe, and Judah was also the name of one of the sons of Jacob, whose father was Isaac, whose father was Abraham. Abraham was the one to whom the Lord God promised this land. His descendants are the ones who live in it." I paused and glared. "I know your stories."

Melchi clicked her tongue again. She stared at me, obviously trying to make up her mind whether it was a good idea to keep on talking to a Moabite.

"So what is Naomi going to do?" she asked eventually. "Most of her relatives are dead. The famine was bad for all of Elimelek's family—even those who *didn't* run away from Israel."

My heart sank.

Melchi smiled. "She doesn't know, does she? She

doesn't know what she's going to do. She'll end up a beggar, just you watch. Cursed by the Lord. And you with her."

I pursed my lips. I did *not* want us to become beggars. And this woman was obviously not inclined to be helpful, but she was my only hope right now.

"Can you point us to somewhere to stay?" I asked, trying to arrange my face to make it friendly and open.

She curled her lip. "Nowhere that will want a Moabite."

When I got back to Naomi, she was still hunched over by the wall. I took a deep breath, dropped down next to her, and showed her the bread. Food would need to come first, and *then* a conversation.

She reached out a wrinkled hand and broke off a piece, then put it in her mouth and chewed. I leaned back against the wall and ate my own portion of the loaf. It was a little dry, but tasty.

I waited until Naomi had finished eating, and then I waited a bit more. The food needed time to get to her belly and make her feel better.

At last Naomi shifted her position and raised her head to look at me. "There is nobody."

"There's… nobody?"

"There is no one who will help us." She nodded at the house opposite, the one where a woman had looked out through a window. "That was the house of Elimelek's brother. I knocked on the door while you were gone."

"And…?"

"Elimelek's brother is dead. He died in the famine. So did his sons. Now someone else lives there."

I took this in. "But there must be other relatives. Other people."

"No." She shook her head. "This town won't welcome us, not after all these years. A worn-out old widow and a Moabite girl? We were wrong to come. The Lord has turned against us."

She spoke in a flat, expressionless voice. When she'd finished, she settled back against the wall again with an air of finality.

I gritted my teeth.

"All right." There wasn't any point in fighting her, I knew that. "All right. We'll have to knock on doors. Ask around. *Someone* will let us stay with them. Israel is supposed to be a place of generosity, for goodness' sake."

Naomi looked at me in amazement as I jumped to my feet and held out my hand to her.

"I don't know if it's true that the Lord has turned against us," I said, "but I do know that we are *not* giving up!"

CHAPTER 12

I Need Your Help

It took less time than I had feared: the potter agreed to let us sleep in his house. I could tell that his wife was not at all enthusiastic about this, but I didn't care; the main thing was, we had somewhere to stay.

Naomi was so annoyed at me for sorting this out that she refused to speak to me all evening. She actually seemed to *want* to give up on life and crumble into dust. But I wanted to live!

"Let me go to the fields," I said to Naomi the following day.

She looked at me mournfully.

"I'll pick up the leftover grain. Maybe there'll be someone who shows me some favour."

She turned her head away.

"Naomi?"

"Go ahead, my daughter," came her muffled, listless voice.

That was good enough for me. I scarpered before she could change her mind.

The fields started as soon as I left the town. On the steeper slopes the land had been cut into steps, so that the whole hillside looked like a giant staircase. They'd done something to channel water onto each step, so the stairs were bright green with thriving plants: in a few months there would be beans and grapes, cucumbers and fat green olives. But I wasn't interested in any of that, hungry though the sight made me. I was heading for the barley fields.

I found a path and followed it around the edge of the town wall. The fields I'd seen when we arrived must be on the other side of Bethlehem, where the ground was flatter. Yes! I could hear the familiar papery rustle of ripe barley stalks. I could see the yellow-brown fields, and the bent backs of the harvesters scattered all across them.

But which field to choose? There were dozens of the rough rectangles squeezed onto the uneven hillside. I climbed up onto a pile of stones to get a better look. Should I try one of the bigger fields, on the basis that the harvesters there would have more to be generous with, if they did let me glean? Or should I choose a smaller field where there were only one or two people to complain about my presence?

I still couldn't quite believe that this gleaning thing was really true—that I could just gather the dropped stalks freely and nobody would chase me away. But Mahlon had told me more than once that that was how they did things in Israel. At least, that was how they were *supposed* to do things.

A man in the nearest field was scowling at me. Not here, then. I hopped off my stones and made a gesture of respect, then walked on. I re-wrapped my headscarf so that it covered part of my face.

The next field had only young men in it. One of them nudged another as I approached and said something I couldn't hear, then they both looked at me with cruel smiles. One of them put a hand on the cudgel in his belt, and looked like he was considering coming over to me. My heart raced.

A line of fruit trees hid the next set of fields. I ran towards it, hoping and praying that those men wouldn't follow.

The path became a wiggle that took me down a steep rocky section to a broader, flatter patch of land. The fields were more regular here, with lots of workers. Stones had been carefully arranged in lines to mark one plot from the next, and there was a series of small wooden platforms where the overseers stood watch. This was the really good land, I could tell; the plots were big and the barley grew tall and straight. Bundles of cut grain already stood at the edges of each one.

The men from beyond the fruit trees weren't following me. Good. I breathed out, and then in, slowly.

Come on then, Ruth, I said to myself, *just pick a field. Just try one.*

But which?

Please, I said in my head, as if the gods were listening. *Please help.*

Then I thought, maybe he *is* listening. The God of Israel. The kind God. Maybe, just maybe, Naomi is wrong, and he hasn't turned against us. Maybe he'll take pity on us.

"Lord God," I prayed out loud, "I know I'm a Moabite, and not really part of your people, but if you would be willing, I need your help. Take me to the right field. A field where I can find favour and be safe."

And I walked forwards.

I went to the overseer's platform first. "Sir," I said humbly, still hiding most of my face, "may I glean behind the reapers?"

The man looked down at me in surprise. "Who are you?" Then his eyes widened. "You must be that Moabite girl. The one who's come back with Naomi. Aren't you? My wife told me about you."

I nodded once, my heart beating fast. "May I glean, sir? Just there among the sheaves, behind the harvesters?

I won't take anything from the sheaves themselves."

"I should hope not." He looked me up and down. "Go on, then. Glean. Though, the master may tell you to get lost when he comes down here later."

He gestured towards the harvesters. "OY!" he shouted across the field. "This girl's going to glean! Let her!"

The harvesters straightened up for a moment, glanced over at me, then bent again to their work.

I hurried to my own.

Only a small part of the field had been reaped so far. Two men were swinging their sickles again and again through the crop, cutting it from left to right so that it fell into a long heap next to where they'd walked. The other harvesters followed behind to gather the barley straws into small sheaves. There were two young women at the back of the line who were picking up the sheaves and leaning them against each other to form upright stacks.

I gulped. This team of harvesters looked efficient. How much dropped grain was I really going to be able to gather?

But if you try another field, I reasoned with myself, *they might not even let you glean at all.*

And maybe, maybe the God of Israel had led me to this one for a reason.

I knelt down at the edge of the field, feeling the cut-off stalks prickle at my knees, and bent forwards to comb through them with my hands. I couldn't see a single scrap of grain. But I had no choice. I would just have to be methodical, working my way through every tiny patch and not letting any part of the field go unchecked.

I shuffled forward on my hands and knees, slowly and painfully moving across the edge of the field. Here was a bit of barley—I grabbed it. There was another. Here was a beetle waggling its feelers at me; it flew away on bright blue wings.

By the time I'd reached the other side of the field, I had a small fistful of barley-stalks with maybe twenty individual grains clinging to them. It was a start.

I picked one grain with care and put it on my tongue. I rolled it around my mouth, then cracked down on the kernel with my teeth so that I could taste the goodness inside. It was a little bitter and a little sweet.

This is going to work, I told myself. *You're going to make it work.*

I put my tiny pile of stalks down carefully on the bare earth at the edge of the field, turned around, and started making my way on my hands and knees back to the other side.

CHAPTER 13

The Master

In the middle of the morning, I allowed myself a little rest.

There was a rough shelter made of branches by the side of the field, opposite the guard's platform. Big water jars had been placed there, and occasionally one of the workers would go over to fill a cup, refresh themselves, and sit in the shade for a few moments. I had told myself that when I got to a certain point in the field, I could go over there too and enjoy being out of the sun.

But I wouldn't go at the same time as anyone else. I wanted to avoid the harvesters, especially the men with their sharp sickles. I had nobody to protect me—no father or brother or husband to fight for me. And I was pretty sure that everyone in the field must realise that. So they would also know that if they wanted to make my life difficult, nobody would stop them.

Just keep quiet and don't annoy anyone, I told myself shakily, *and things will go well.*

When I finally got to the point in the field that I had marked out in my head, some of the harvesters were in the shelter. Cursing inwardly, I kept my head down and focused on the field until at last I heard the overseer shout, "Back to work, boys, you've had long enough!"

I felt dizzy with relief.

As the workers made their way back into the barley, I pulled a couple of black threads out of my headscarf and tied them round the tiny stack I'd gathered, to mark it as my own. Then I walked over to the shelter, keeping my eyes down, trying to blend into my surroundings and not draw attention to myself.

I didn't dare drink the water from the jars. I'd brought a little skin of my own, though—I tipped my head back and glugged down the water inside. It was warm and a bit sour from being left in the sun, but it was water. I poured a tiny bit onto my hands and carefully wiped my hot face and arms. Then I sat back against a cool rock that formed the base of the shelter at the back, and nibbled the bit of bread I'd brought with me.

Across the field, the overseer nodded at me. Hopefully that meant he didn't mind me sitting here.

I wondered who his master was. Who was so rich that he not only owned this big field but could also hire all these workers and not even do any harvesting himself? I suddenly worried that when he turned up—which the overseer had said he would—I would be chased away. One of the women had definitely given me an unpleasant look as I'd walked past her and the other workers. She'd be glad to see the back of me, I was sure. And why shouldn't she? I was the lowest of the low. I had nothing. I wasn't even a hired servant like she was. I was just a dirty, poor foreigner who nobody cared about.

Hopefully the master would take his time in coming down.

I rested as long as I dared, which wasn't very long, and then shuffled back across the field to keep on working. This time the men stopped their work and openly stared at me as I went. I tried to ignore them.

"The Lord be with you!"

"The Lord bless you, sir."

"May God bless you, sir!"

I straightened up as the shouts rippled across the field. The woman closest to me was curtseying. The men with the sickles had put them down to raise their hands in greeting. All of them were focused on a newcomer, who was standing among them with a big grin on his face.

"May the Lord bless you, sir," another of the workers said, clasping the newcomer on his arm. "How goes it?"

"Oh, well, business as usual," laughed the newcomer. He looked around at the harvest. "You're making good

progress here, praise God. Let me just speak to the overseer and then I'll come and join you."

"Yes, sir." The men hefted their curved sickles again.

I watched the newcomer pace across the field, taking
care not to disturb the fresh stacks of barley. He was a
thickset, strong-looking man, but not young—there was
grey in his reddish beard. He wore good-quality boots
and a well-made coat over his tunic.

There was no doubt about it: this was the master. The
rich, rich man who owned this field.

Hastily I bent over again, feverishly searching the
ground for bits of barley. There was one! I added it to
my fistful and crawled forward another hand's-breadth.
Then another. Then another. *Keep your head down, Ruth.*

But it was too late—I had already attracted his attention.

"Who does that young woman belong to?" The master's voice was loud and floated easily over to me from
the overseer's platform.

"She's the Moabite…" I heard the overseer say, but the
rest of his sentence was snatched away.

Next I heard footsteps crackling through the field
again. *Keep gleaning,* I told myself, gritting my teeth.
*Don't look up. Don't draw attention. Just get as much as
you can before they make you stop.*

Another patch of ground. Another scrap of barley. Another patch of ground. Another scrap of barley.

I heard the master's voice, quieter this time, talking to

the harvesters. I wished I could hear what the instructions were. *It doesn't matter,* I told myself. *Keep gleaning.*

Another patch of ground. Another square of broken stalks, this time without any grain on them.

Then footsteps came close to me. A man's footsteps, coming heavy and fast through the stubbly field.

I looked up.

The master stood in front of me, not too close. He had a nose just like Mahlon's, I noticed—thin and straight. Not stubby like Naomi's was, or like Kilion's had been.

"I'm Boaz," he said simply. "I hear you've been working in my field all morning."

"Sir…"

"No, don't worry!" he cried, seeing my fear. He waved his hands eagerly. "Listen to me. You're *welcome*. Don't go and glean in another field and don't go away from here. Stay here with the women who work for me." He jerked his head towards the harvesters. "Watch the field where the men are harvesting, and follow along after the women. Don't be afraid. I've told the men they are not to lay a hand on you."

He gave a broad smile. "Oh, and whenever you're thirsty, go and get a drink from the water jars the men have filled. It's no problem."

I gaped.

I was shaking.

I leaned forward, bowing down and pressing my forehead to the earth. The deepest bow I'd ever made. "Sir,"

I said formally, "I'm a foreigner. Why have I found such favour in your eyes?"

"I've been told all about you," Boaz answered. "All about what you've done for your mother-in-law since the death of your husband. How you left your father and mother, and your whole homeland, and came to live with a people you didn't know before."

His voice sounded genuinely admiring.

I straightened up. This was really real, then. It was going to be all right. He was practically saying I could act like one of his own workers—drinking their water, using their shelter, following close behind them.

I met his gaze with a grin.

"May the Lord repay you for what you've done," Boaz said warmly. "May you be richly rewarded by the God of Israel. You've come to him for shelter. You've come under his wings."

You've come under his wings... Then Boaz didn't think that the Lord had cursed us. In fact, he thought the opposite.

I bowed my head.

"Sir," I told him, "you've put me at ease by speaking kindly. I'm your servant. I mean, I don't even have the status of one of your servants... But you're being so kind."

Boaz only chuckled, waved his hand again as if to dismiss what I'd said, and paced away.

CHAPTER 14

Under His Wings

At noon, another servant of Boaz's arrived, a woman carrying loaves of bread and jars of oil and vinegar. The workers all went to the shelter and the overseer handed out cups and bowls. I hung back, but Boaz beckoned to me.

"Come over here," he shouted cheerfully. "Have some bread." He thrust a big loaf into my hands, and pulled me towards the woman with the oil. "Dip it in the wine vinegar. It's good!"

I broke a bit off and sopped it into the bowl of vinegar the woman had poured out. It *was* good—the bread was fluffy and the vinegar sharp. I ate more, and then more.

"Here's some water," Boaz said, drawing me a cup. "Would you like some roasted grain?"

He handed me another bowl and poured the cooked barley into it from a sack. "Have as much as you want. It's good!"

Everything seemed to be good from Boaz's perspective. I felt good too, like he'd warmed me up inside. I tucked in, and ate until I felt fuller than I'd felt in weeks.

I repeated Boaz's words in my head. *The God of Israel. You've come to him for shelter. You've come under his wings.*

When I was very small, Dinah owned a hen named Beautiful, who had four chicks. I used to watch the chicks potter around near their mother, never going too far. I loved those chicks. I used to proudly count them every time I saw them: one, two, three, four.

But one time, I could only see three chicks.

I could still remember how upset I'd been. What could have happened to that last little chick that had seemed so healthy the day before? Had it been eaten? Had it been stolen? Had it got lost? Had its mother abandoned it? I stumbled towards Beautiful, the hen, and squatted down in front of her on my little legs, bawling my eyes out.

Then Dinah found me. "Ruthy, you don't need to cry," she said gently. "Look. The little chick is just under here."

She put out a hand and patted the mother hen, feeling her wings and her breast-feathers. And all of a sudden, a little head popped out. The fourth chick! It had been hidden inside its mother's feathers the whole time, perfectly safe. It was sheltering under her wings.

The God of Israel. You've come to him for shelter. You've come under his wings. Those were Boaz's words.

I knew the God of Israel was supposed to be kind to his people. And I knew he was powerful. But I hadn't ever thought of him like *that*. Like a mother hen. Like a mother hen who might welcome a chick that wasn't even her own, and let it nestle underneath her feathers for warmth and shelter.

Could a god be so kind as *that*?

Yet, as I munched yet another mouthful of food and watched Boaz roar with laughter, I began to believe it.

Boaz's servants were definitely less efficient in the afternoon than they had been in the morning. There was far more grain being left behind as they gathered their bundles, and therefore far more grain for me to pick up. I was pretty sure that some of the women had even taken some stalks from their own sheaves and strewn them across the field just for me. Had Boaz told them to do it? Was he really that generous?

Whatever the reason, the fact was that by the time the sun began to fade, I had gleaned a *lot* of grain. Far too much for me to be able to carry it all back to the potter's house. I would need to separate the grain from the stalks right there beside the field. Which meant threshing.

In order to thresh grain properly, you really need to have a proper threshing floor that's been designed for the purpose, rather than just using any old piece of flat ground. It would also be better to have a proper flail, rather than any old stick. But these things were not available to me. I was going to have to improvise.

The strip of land by the edge of the field looked just about flat and wide enough. I kicked away the stones scattered across it, sweeping my sandals along the ground to make it as smooth as I could. I picked up one of my stacks of barley and dropped it in the middle, arranging it so that all the stalks were pointing out, and all the grain was in the centre. Now it was ready to thresh. All I needed was a makeshift flail to beat the barley grains from their stalks.

Before I could even start looking for one, Boaz was beside me.

"Here, how's this?" He handed me a thick stick that he must have cut from a tree especially. "Tomorrow I'll get someone to bring a proper flail for you. But will this do for today?"

I couldn't make eye contact with him—I just couldn't. Instead I took the stick and hefted it in my hands. It was a good stick.

"Thank you, sir."

"No problem. Look, I meant what I said earlier. Don't go to another field. You can stay with my workers until they've finished harvesting all my grain. The wheat as well as the barley."

He was looking out into the field, shielding his eyes against the low sun, as his servants finished their work and gathered their belongings to go home. It was the gaze of a man who was satisfied with what he had.

"Sir," I said softly, "are you always this generous?"

He turned to me with sparkling eyes and a broad grin. "Well, I don't often meet—"

But he stopped, suddenly distracted. He'd spotted something behind me—no, someone. He smacked his palm on his forehead.

"That messenger is coming for me. I'm sorry. I've just remembered—I've got to go!"

He backed away and jogged towards the messenger coming down the hillside. I turned and watched him go.

"He's like that," came a woman's voice behind me. "Boaz. He's a busy man."

It was one of Boaz's workers: a young woman with small features and soft dark eyebrows that touched in the middle. She smiled at me. "Today was a rare day. He doesn't often come and work in the field for the whole afternoon."

"He puts a lot of trust in his servants," I said, "to do their work well without him there."

She nodded. "He chooses carefully."

Then she looked at me curiously. "He's obviously impressed by *you*. All that grain…"

"Did he tell you to pull bits out so that I could glean more?" I asked.

"Yes, he did. Not a very usual request from a man who makes his money from what he harvests in the field."

She paused. Then, as if making up her mind, she put a hand on my shoulder. "I'm Iscah. My husband isn't sure about you, since you're a Moabite. But if Boaz likes you, then so do I."

"Iscah," I repeated, smiling. "I'm Ruth."

Then I sighed. "I'd better thresh this grain. It'll be dark before long."

CHAPTER 15

Thief!

By the time I reached the potter's house, it was entirely dark. Mercifully, the night was cloudless and a bright moon had lit my way. I'd made it through the darkness unharmed and without getting lost. But it was late. Much too late.

The potter's door was barred from the inside. I leaned against it tiredly for a moment, then bashed my fist against the wood. "It's Ruth! The Moabite! Let me in!"

Silence.

Then I heard a scrabble from inside and a thud as the bar was removed. The door creaked open just a crack, then widened slightly to reveal the potter's wife.

"You're alive!" she remarked.

I raised my eyebrows. "Can I come in?"

"We thought you must have run off, maybe," the potter's wife said as she opened the door fully. "Or been *taken*." She seemed to take great delight in this thought. "Your mother-in-law has been worried sick."

But all I could think was that I was desperate to get rid of the weight I was carrying. The walk from Boaz's field had felt like a very long way. I heaved the bundle of grain onto the floor with a groan, and flopped down next to it. My whole body ached. Every single muscle.

"Well, I'm back now," I said. "Could I have a cup of water?"

"How dare you flop on my floor like that—" began the potter's wife angrily. But she trailed off. "What have you got in that bundle? Is that all—"

I lay my head back and closed my eyes. "It's all grain, yes."

I heard the woman fiddle with the bundle, untying my knot to check what was inside. She gasped audibly. Then she slapped my cheek, hard.

"Thief! You must be a thief! I knew I should never let a filthy Moabite into my house—you'll bring shame on my family—I want you out at once—how dare you steal from the good, honest people of Ephrathah—your father-in-law would turn in his grave if he knew—"

I sat up, wincing. "No! No! Stop! I didn't steal it. I didn't steal it. It's mine. I gleaned it. I gathered it all."

The potter's wife stared at me.

Naomi, appearing from the shadowy corner of the room, stared too.

"I gathered it all," I repeated, "on my hands and knees. I went to the field of a kind man who let me glean. He gave me food. He told his workers to leave some of the barley so that I would have lots to pick up. That's how I've got so much. I didn't steal."

The potter's wife looked at Naomi.

"My daughter-in-law is no thief," my mother-in-law said. She knelt down creakily and ran her hands through the grain. "Ruth," she said in a shaky voice, "where did you glean? Where did you work? In whose field? Blessed be the man who took notice of you!"

"His name was Boaz," I told her.

"Boaz!" exclaimed the potter's wife.

"Boaz!" whispered Naomi. "May the Lord bless him!"

"Yes," I agreed. "Now please may I have a cup of water?"

After I'd drunk and washed, Naomi patted the cushion next to her to invite me to sit. She wasn't refusing to speak to me anymore, then. I had no complaint; I sat beside her and leaned on her bony shoulder like a child with its mother.

Naomi stroked my hair for a moment. Then, swallowing, she whispered, "Ruth, the Lord has not stopped showing his kindness, to the living and the dead."

A tear dropped from her eye onto my nose.

I squeezed her hand, happy that she didn't feel cursed any more. "You're right. You've always told me that your

God is kind, haven't you? He hasn't turned away from us after all."

Then I caught up fully with what she'd said. "What do you mean, he's shown kindness to the living and *the dead*?"

"That man, Boaz," she croaked, "he's our kinsman. He's one of our redeemers."

I didn't know what a redeemer was, or why this meant that the Lord had showed kindness to the dead. But I was used to Naomi making statements that she didn't bother to explain. I'd find out eventually.

What I *was* interested in was the word "kinsman".

I straightened up and looked my mother-in-law in the eyes. "Our kinsman. Our relative. I thought you said you didn't have any of those left."

Her eyes were still tear-filled. She shook her head wordlessly.

"Naomi, do you think Boaz would take us in? If we're family?"

The potter's wife scoffed from across the room. "Ha! Boaz?! He's not *that* closely related to you." She sneered. "And he's not married. He couldn't take a young woman like you into his house—it wouldn't be right. Not unless he married you, and why on earth would he do that? He's one of the richest and most respected men in Bethlehem. You should be grateful for what you've had from him already—which is more than anybody else would give! And not ask for anything more."

There was silence for a moment.

I was still looking at Naomi. "He told me to stay with his workers until they finish harvesting all his grain. The wheat as well as the barley."

She nodded. "That will be good. In someone else's field you might be harmed. Stay with the women who work for Boaz."

That was all she said. But before I leant back onto her shoulder, I saw that she had a little smile on her face. A secretive, I've-got-a-plan sort of smile.

I was too tired to ask questions. I'd just do as I was told. The barley harvest, then the wheat harvest. And then we'd see.

CHAPTER 16

The Harvesters

The following day felt entirely different. I walked out of the house with a smile on my face, marching confidently through the fields until I reached Boaz's plot. It already felt familiar and friendly. I waved at Iscah, the girl who'd introduced herself the evening before, and she waved back cheerily. Then I settled down to glean with a sense of purpose. I even hummed to myself as I worked.

And things only got better.

It started with Iscah. She followed me to the shelter when I went to take my rest in the middle of the morning, and gave me a shy smile.

"You sit down—I'll draw the water," she said, holding out her hand for my cup.

Soon the two of us were sitting side by side in the shade, looking out across the field.

"Everyone's talking about you, you know," Iscah said.

"People are very curious. Most widows who are still young would go back to live with their parents, and hope to get married again. Not follow their mother-in-law to a foreign country where they don't belong."

"Well," I answered cautiously, "I married into Naomi's family, didn't I? I couldn't just go back on that and abandon her. I'm her daughter-in-law. She needed me."

"But what are you going to *do*?"

"I'm going to look after my mother-in-law."

"But who's going to look after *you*?" she replied, sitting up and looking at me seriously. "It's a hard life, being a widow. Don't you want to get married again? And have children?"

"I've only just got here. The Lord God has been kind so far. I'm going to keep gleaning while the harvest lasts, and then I'll see."

Iscah looked unsure about that, but she wasn't the type to argue.

"Look," she said softly, "the other women are coming. Don't worry, they're all right."

It seemed that all three of the other female harvesters had decided to take their break too. They crowded into the shelter, drawing water for themselves and fanning their faces with their hands. Iscah scooched up into the corner to leave space, and I did the same.

"Go on, then, Iscah, introduce us," said a heavyset woman with a large chin, staring at me pointedly.

Iscah had told me not to worry, but this was *definitely* the woman who had scowled at me on the first day.

"This is Ruth," Iscah answered softly. "She's the Moabite—"

"—who came back with Naomi. Yes, we all know *that*," said the woman.

But she seemed to be waiting for something else.

"Um, and this is Keziah, wife of Toran," said Iscah, gesturing from me to her.

The heavyset woman—Keziah—nodded at me, obviously pleased with the formality of this introduction.

"And I'm Hagabah," said the woman just behind Keziah, leaning forwards enthusiastically.

"And I'm Ahinoam," added the third woman, who wore a pink dress and had wooden earrings in her earlobes.

I smiled faintly, not quite trusting them yet.

Abruptly, Keziah said, "I remember those boys from when they were little. Sweet things."

I stared at her.

"I mean Mahlon and Kilion," she clarified impatiently. "Kilion followed his brother everywhere. They looked just the same as each other, except for their age. Same eyes, same mouth. The only thing that was different was—"

"Their noses," I murmured, saying it at the same time as the older woman.

She looked astonished.

"Kilion's was just like Naomi's," I said, "but Mahlon's was the same as his father's."

"Yes, that's right," she replied.

"When did they die?" asked Hagabah in a hushed voice, still leaning forward from behind Keziah.

I swallowed. "Two months ago."

"What was he like?" asked Hagabah, still in a hushed voice. "Your husband?"

"He was…" I hesitated, wanting to do him justice. "He was hard-working. He was always ready to work. And kind—he was kind. He was good at looking after people."

My eyes were moist. Why did they have to ask about this?

But it seemed to have won me their approval.

"*You're* hard-working too," Hagabah observed. "A blessing to Naomi. She's fortunate to have you."

"She's fortunate to have *Boaz*," corrected Ahinoam sarcastically.

No one could disagree. They all fell silent as they contemplated their wealthy master.

"He seems a good man," I ventured.

"Oh, yes," Keziah said loyally. "*There's* a man who stands up for the Lord's ways."

I hesitated. "It seems… not everyone in Bethlehem does? I saw a shrine when we first arrived…"

"That was destroyed years ago," asserted Keziah, "after the famine. We turned back to the Lord. There is no place for other gods in Ephrathah now."

"Well, there is in some households," cut in Ahinoam in an amused voice, her wooden earrings clacking slightly as she shook her head.

"But the owners of those households don't boast about it," responded Keziah with a glare. She turned back to me, looking a little dangerous again. "I suppose you're a worshipper of all sorts of gods. Being a Moabite."

"No, actually," I said.

Keziah's nostrils flared in surprise.

"We worshipped all sorts of gods, you're right," I went on, "when I was growing up. But when I met Naomi… her God was different."

"Different how?" whispered Iscah.

"Your God has done things that our gods would never do," I replied, suddenly feeling confident. "*Could* never do, maybe. We would pray to Chemosh for a good harvest, or, I don't know, victory in battle. We would ask the gods to make things go well, and hope that they did. But your God actually wants to help his people. He has a *plan*. And he really *does* things. Next to him, our gods are… well, you'd hardly even call them gods."

I fell silent, amazed at what I'd just said. But it was true—I did believe it.

"That's right," said Keziah in a satisfied tone. "Our Lord is a miracle-working God. When our people were slaves, far away in Egypt, he set us free. He parted the sea to let the Israelites through it, and made the waves crash over the soldiers who were chasing after them. He brought us to our own land. He—"

"He's *kind*," I interrupted.

I didn't need to hear those stories about God's rescue of his people. I was already feeling surer about this than I'd ever felt before. He was kind, this God of Israel. He actually seemed to care! He actually loved his people— and if what Boaz had said was right, he might even love *me* as well. Even though I was a Moabite.

"I haven't come here to worship the Moabite gods," I concluded. "Like I say, they're nothing in comparison. I've come here to worship the Lord. I've come under his wings for refuge."

I was silently daring the women to disagree. But they mainly looked impressed. Keziah even took my hand in hers and squeezed it.

"May the Lord continue to show you kindness," she said.

So they accepted me, and by some miracle it was easy. And they also carried on following Boaz's instructions to pull out the bits of grain especially so that I could pick them up. So once again, by the end of the day I had an enormous quantity of barley to thresh and take home.

And that was when Boaz turned up again.

CHAPTER 17

Not Slaves *Yet*

He was carrying a flail: a pole about as long as my arm, with a thicker stick attached to the end that would hit the barley with force when I swung it. He came whistling down the path with it over his shoulder, and waved at me enthusiastically as soon as he spotted me.

Iscah and Ahinoam, who were close by, followed me to meet him.

"I've brought you what I promised," Boaz said, handing me the flail. "My own grain will all be threshed at the end of the harvest, so you can borrow this until then."

He looked at the stacks of grain just behind me. "Oh good. You've been able to gather plenty."

"Thanks to you, sir," I said.

Boaz beamed. Well—he didn't grin exactly, not this time. His mouth twitched, but it was his eyes that shone. It was like his whole face was bursting with kindness, and his eyes were the only place where it could get out. They had deep crinkles around the edges.

"How is your mother-in-law?" he asked quietly.

"She is well, thank you, sir."

"Really well? The journey to Bethlehem didn't exhaust her?"

I hesitated. "Well, yes, it did. She's old. It was harder for her than it was for me. But she'll be all right. It was… Sir, it did her a lot of good to hear about your kindness to me yesterday."

He did that eye-beam thing again. "Look after her, Ruth."

I bowed.

But the interview wasn't over. When I straightened up, Boaz was looking at me thoughtfully, seriously, as if he was trying to puzzle something out. "Did Naomi tell you that I'm a relative of hers? Of her husband's, actually. Not a close relative, but part of the same clan."

"Yes, sir. Is that why you—why you've been so kind?"

He nodded slowly. "Yes. Well, that and other reasons." He spread his hands to indicate the fields around us. "When our people entered this land—even before they arrived, actually—the Lord God told us that widows and orphans and foreigners must be looked after. Grain is supposed be left for them to glean. Food is supposed be sold to them at a reasonable price. These things have been God's law from the beginning, but too many of my countrymen ignore them." He looked at me steadily.

"I'm glad the Lord led you to *my* field."

Then it was his turn to give a little bow, as if I was worthy of his respect. And he went off to greet the other workers.

Ahinoam and Iscah crowded round me immediately.

"He's related to your father-in-law?" exclaimed Ahinoam. "He's your kinsman?"

"Apparently so," I said.

"That explains it all!" she cried. "I *thought* it was strange how well he was treating you."

I thought back to Naomi's words the day before. "Naomi said he was… something beginning with R."

"A redeemer," Iscah said quietly.

"Do you not have those in Moab?" asked Ahinoam. Her earrings clacked as she shook her head pityingly.

"What is a redeemer?" I asked, confused.

"It's…" Iscah began. "How can I explain it?" She ran a finger up and down her nose thoughtfully, ruffling the hairs at the top where her eyebrows met. "Imagine my husband and I don't work for Boaz. Imagine we farm our own land, but it's poor land and we end up not having enough to eat. So now we have to spend money we don't have, and we get into debt. At that point we have no choice; we have no way of paying the money back. We'll end up selling ourselves into slavery instead. We'll work unpaid for the person we owe money to, until our work has paid off our debt."

"Right."

"So now we're slaves, and there's nothing we can do about it. *But*, along comes a kinsman of ours—my husband's uncle, it would be. He goes to the person we're slaving for, and he hands over all the money we owe. Now our debt is gone. The kinsman has set us free. He's redeemed us."

"Like the Lord setting your ancestors free, when *they* were slaves," I said.

"Exactly."

"But… Naomi and I aren't slaves."

Ahinoam laughed. "You're not *yet*."

Iscah shook her head slightly as if to tell me to ignore this. "A redeemer might also buy land," she explained. "If you have to sell your land, again because you're too poor and you're in debt, then the redeemer is supposed to buy it, to keep it in the family. Because in Israel, every family's land is a gift from God. So they're supposed to keep it."

"But Naomi and I don't have any land," I said.

"Look," cut in Ahinoam, "the point is, a kinsman redeemer is someone who has money, and can spend it on looking after the other people in his family. Usually it's about specific situations like slavery and buying fields, but clearly Boaz is taking it further. He's looking after you even before he has to." Her eyes glinted. "I wonder just how far he'll go."

"What do you mean?" I asked, feeling stupid, but she shook her head and gave a secret smile. It was just like the one Naomi had given me the day before.

I made it back to the potter's house a little earlier that night. On the way, as I came through the gates of the town, I saw that the elders had not gone home yet— they were still sitting underneath the acacia tree. Two men stood in front of them. As I approached, one of them took off a sandal and gave it to the other.

"The purchase is made," intoned one of the elders.

I laughed. Whoever came up with the idea of using sandals to make it official when something had been bought or sold? I was happy to be in Israel, but they did have some strange customs. Like the thing about a man marrying his dead brother's widow. And the Sabbath—a whole day when nobody did any work.

I was still smiling to myself, but suddenly I became aware of a cold silence.

The elders of Bethlehem were all looking at me. All of them.

"Why are you laughing, Moabite girl?" said one of them in a chilly voice. He had a thin face with a narrow, straight nose. An embroidered cap covered his hair.

I shivered in recognition. This was the same man as had stared at us when we first arrived. Who was he? Did he know Naomi? I could feel his dislike—but why did he dislike me? Was it just because I was a Moabite, or was there some other reason?

"I'm sorry," I gabbled, stepping backwards. "I didn't mean—"

"If you want to find a place here," said the man coldly, "you should keep your laughter to yourself."

I scurried away.

CHAPTER 18

Naomi's Secret

After six days of work, we reached a Sabbath, which meant a day of rest. A whole day! I could happily have stayed in bed for hours. There'd be no sweeping, no cooking, no shuffling around in fields… I could just sleep and eat and lie around. Maybe I'd get Naomi to tell me an old story or two.

This was what I was expecting. But Naomi had other plans.

She slapped my cheeks softly to wake me up, though I was only dozing. "Ruth!" she cried. "Come on. I want to show you Ephrathah."

I groaned and twisted away from her. "I've seen Ephrathah. I've been out every day."

"You haven't seen what *I* want to show you. Come on."

I groaned again and rubbed my eyes dramatically. "I'm tired."

But to tell the truth, I was secretly very pleased that Naomi wanted to go out. As far as I knew, she hadn't left the potter's house since we arrived there. She was worn out by the journey here, and by the endless daily work to keep us clothed and clean and fed. But it would be good for her to get out.

"You're not as tired as I am," she declared dismissively. "Come on."

So I got up, and soon the two of us were arm-in-arm, tottering slowly through the quiet Sabbath-morning streets.

I expected her to take me around the town, but instead we went straight towards the gates, past the shady acacia tree, and out towards the fields.

"Naomi," I complained, "I go this way every day. What are you going to show me?"

But she gave no answer.

We didn't go all the way down the hill to the flattest fields, but stayed among the less good plots of land. Naomi led me along the winding tracks that split one small field from another, taking care not to disturb any of the crops as we went. She had to stop for a rest several times. I wished I'd thought to bring water to refresh her.

The fourth time we stopped, it was beside a plot that was small and badly planted. There were as many weeds as barley-stalks, and rocks littered the ground. Some of it had been harvested already, but it was clear that there was only one man working here and he was making slow progress.

Still, the rustle of ripe barley plants in the breeze was a sound I always enjoyed, and the warmth of the sun was starting to make itself known. I sat down happily on a tree stump and waited for Naomi to get her breath back.

"Where are we going?" I asked as her wheezing stopped. "And are you sure you can manage to walk all the way there?"

"*This* is where we're going," she replied. "This is what I wanted to show you."

I looked around again at the meagre field. The rocks, the straggly crops, the weeds. *"This?"*

"This." She nodded. Her eyes were excited. "This field was ours. Elimelek's. And it would have been Mahlon's, if he'd lived."

This was the land they had farmed when they lived in Bethlehem before. I looked around it again, marvelling. Imagining a younger version of Naomi and poor old Elimelek, working hard, just the two of them. And Mahlon and Kilion, two young boys, scampering around while their parents worked.

I swallowed. "So who owns it now?"

"We do. Well, sort of."

"What?" I cried. I couldn't believe it. "This is *our* land? How could you not tell me this?! I assumed you'd sold whatever land you had before you came to Moab."

She looked offended. "Of course not. It's our land. It's been in Elimelek's family for generations. The Lord gave it to us. We would never have sold it." She sniffed. "And, I don't have to tell you everything."

I groaned. "But Naomi… I've been working in Boaz's field all this time. We could have…"

I trailed off as I gestured uselessly at the crops beside us. No, it was much better to glean in Boaz's field than to harvest *this*.

And anyway, somebody else had planted all of this, and that same someone would be harvesting it. Whoever it was might have been planting here for ten years. It had been Elimelek's land once, but it wasn't anymore, surely.

But Naomi didn't agree. "This is the family inheritance," she said firmly. "It was Elimelek's, and it was his father's before him, and his grandfather's. It should have been Mahlon's, and then Mahlon's son's."

"But Mahlon and I had no sons. So… who inherits it?"

She shook her head. "Well, we're the last of the family. We have a right to it. But we can't farm it ourselves, not on our own. We have to sell it. Or rather—" her eyes gleamed— "we have to see if someone will *redeem* it."

Naomi's plan was to wait until the harvest was over.

The person who had sown these crops ought to be the one to harvest them. But after that, Naomi would go to the elders and announce that she wanted to reclaim her right to the field. They would agree that it belonged to Elimelek's family, and then they would appeal for men from the same clan to come forward to redeem it. The man who came forward would buy the field, which meant it would stay in the clan, even though Elimelek's family line had effectively died out. (Naomi and I still counted in the family line, but we were widows—there weren't going to be any more children.) And we would get money, which we desperately needed.

"Everyone wins," Naomi concluded.

It sounded good at first. Especially since the person Naomi was hoping would redeem it was Boaz. He would give us a good price—he might even overpay. He seemed eager to make sure Naomi and I were all right.

But what about after that? The money would run out eventually.

The thought of having land of our own had made me so excited for a moment. We could grow our own crops! Make our own decisions! Have some control over our lives again! And we wouldn't be beggars; we'd be land-owners. Even if the land we owned was not very good, it did mean we'd be treated with more respect. We'd be proper Israelites: part of God's people, owning a small part of his promised land.

But Naomi was right: we couldn't work the land just the two of us.

So we'd sell it… and then we'd spend the money on keeping ourselves alive. How long would it last—a year perhaps? And then we'd be poor again, and even worse off than before.

I shivered. "Naomi, I'm scared."

But my mother-in-law just smiled. "Trust me," she said. "Trust the Lord."

CHAPTER 19

The Problem with the Future

As the weeks passed, the fields all around Bethlehem turned ugly. The swaying, rustling grain was cut down, one small swathe at a time, until it was all gone. Just the stubble was left: thousands of dry, headless stalks, sticking up from the ground like a memorial for the dead.

Except of course they were really a sign of the living—of food that would keep bellies full and bodies working.

During those weeks I alternated between two moods. Sometimes I was overcome with gratitude: I was in Israel, the land promised by God to his people, and I believed in this God and felt welcomed by him. It felt like I was somewhere special. And I was grateful to Boaz, and to Iscah and the other women in the field. On those days, I wandered about with a precious sense of wonder, like I'd found a beautiful pearl and was carrying it close to my chest.

But other times I felt black and despairing. The work was hard and the days were long. Even with all Boaz's generosity, I was still a poor widow and an outsider, with no obvious future. On those days I grumped at Naomi, got irritated by Iscah, and clomped around feeling certain that my body would always ache and I would never find a real home ever again.

There were seven weeks of the barley harvest, and seven weeks of the wheat harvest. During those fourteen weeks I worked harder than I had ever done in my life. And then it was almost over.

On the final day of the wheat harvest, Iscah wasn't there. I felt bad because I'd snapped at her about something the previous day, and I wanted to apologise. She hadn't missed a single day of work so far—what could be wrong?

I considered going up to her husband to ask him. But I'd kept my distance from Boaz's male servants all harvest, and it felt too strange to change that now.

Fortunately Ahinoam, who loved to gossip, knew exactly what had happened.

"She's pregnant," she whispered to me when the midday break came. "Been throwing up every morning—her husband told my husband. It's a sure sign. She'll give birth this winter. It's her first one."

A child. A real family! I felt a pang of jealousy, which Ahinoam immediately spotted.

"If you want a child, you'll have to get married again," she said matter-of-factly. She nodded towards the men, who were all sitting or standing on the other side of the shelter. Two of the men were older, as old as Boaz: Keziah's husband Toran, and Ahinoam's own husband, who had a big black beard and an old scar running all down one arm. Boaz was there as well, as good-humoured as ever. Then there were three others: Azzan, the husband of Iscah, plus Joram and Ozias, who were both unmarried.

To my horror, Ahinoam grabbed my shoulders and started pushing me towards them.

"Go on. Just try saying hello; that's all you have to do. Let them know you're available. Who knows what might happen?"

But I fought her off, twisting out of her grip like I'd twisted out of my mother's when I was a child. "I don't want to marry them," I hissed at her angrily. "Leave me alone."

She looked annoyed. "But Ruth, you're being stupid. What kind of future do you have without a husband?"

"I have to stay with Naomi," I muttered. "I can't get married."

Ahinoam tutted. "You're too loyal to that woman. What has she ever given you? She's a complete misery as far as I heard."

I shook my head, biting my tongue to stop myself from arguing back, and pulled away. I'd take my food and stand outside the shelter instead; there was a tree there to give me some shade. I stood facing away from the harvesters, rubbed my eyes to get rid of the tears, and shoved some bread in my mouth. Then I chewed it angrily.

The truth was, we were both right. The only way I could guarantee my future would be if I had a son. The only way I could have a son would be if I married again. But I couldn't marry again without abandoning Naomi—which I had sworn never to do.

If she had had another son, I could have married *him*—that way I'd stay in the family. But she didn't. Mahlon and Kilion were both dead. And—as Naomi had said to me when we first left for Israel—even if she were young enough to get married again and have another child, I was hardly going to wait for him to grow up and then marry a boy more than twenty years younger than me.

So what was I supposed to do?

As I finished my mouthful, I heard footsteps crunching across the stubble towards me.

I whirled around angrily. "Ahinoam, I told you, leave me alone!"

But it wasn't Ahinoam. It was Boaz.

He looked taken aback: people like me did not speak to people like him like that.

"Sir, I'm so sorry—" I began to stutter, but he shook his head to stop me. He had a strange expression on his face.

"I…" He hesitated. "I'm sorry for your distress."

I felt my cheeks go bright red. Had he overheard the conversation with Ahinoam? What must he think?

"I admire your loyalty to your mother-in-law," he said very softly.

I pressed my lips together, not knowing what to say.

Boaz swallowed. He opened his mouth as if to say something. Then he changed his mind and shut it again. His eyes weren't beaming now—they looked upset, as if he was pleading with me to do something. To say something.

So I said, "It's good news that Iscah is pregnant."

"Oh yes," he said, with apparent relief. "I hope it will be the first of many."

"And a son," I said, "to continue the family line."

Boaz nodded. "We have a prayer that we pray in Israel when a couple gets married. We pray that the Lord will make the woman like Rachel and Leah, who together built up the house of Israel. Perhaps you know their story?"

"Yes. They were the wives of Jacob, the grandson of Abraham. Jacob's sons became the fathers of the twelve tribes of Israel."

"But there are no sons without mothers," Boaz smiled. "And the mothers of the twelve tribes were Rachel and

Leah. So that's what we pray for every new wife—that she'd be like them. That the Lord will bless the family through her—and bless our whole people, actually. We pray that through her, God's plans will be fulfilled."

I swallowed. Naomi had not prayed that for me when I'd married Mahlon. And she had not prayed it for Orpah when she'd married Kilion. Well, we weren't Israelites—perhaps it wouldn't have been right.

We weren't blessings to the family. We were curses.

It was my turn to look awkward.

But Boaz, seeming self-conscious, was glancing back at the harvesters. By now they were all watching us curiously. Boaz cleared his throat and bowed. "Have you eaten enough? It's almost time to go back to work."

"Thank you, sir," I answered. "I've had enough." Then I added, "Sir, thank you. Thank you for your kindness. If I hadn't come to your fields, I don't know what I would have done. I… I've felt safe here. Under your protection."

He smiled. Then hesitated. "You'd, er, you'd better give me back my flail at the end of today. You won't need it anymore, and my own threshing will start tomorrow, now that the harvest is over."

I nodded. I didn't trust myself to speak.

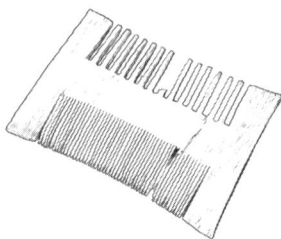

CHAPTER 20

It's Time

"It's time," announced Naomi.

She used such a dramatic tone of voice that I stopped what I was doing and looked up at her.

"Time for what?"

"I've been hoping all this time that Boaz would speak," she told me. "But it seems he isn't going to. So it's time for us to do it."

"To do… what? Do you mean to ask him to redeem the field?"

"No," she said with a wry smile. "I mean, to ask him to marry you."

"To… *what?!*" I dropped the scarf I'd been patching. "What?!" I repeated.

"We need to find a home for you, where you'll be well provided for," Naomi went on, as if I hadn't spoken. "And Boaz, whose women you've worked with, is a relative of ours."

She raised her eyebrows, waiting for it to sink in.

"You want Boaz to marry me?" I said. "Not just to buy the field? Also to marry me? *Me?*"

"Yes."

"Has this been your plan all along?"

"As I said," she replied smugly, without answering my question, "he's a relative of ours."

I had to laugh. *Of course* this had been Naomi's plan all along. This was why she'd been so pleased on that first day when I announced that I'd found my way into Boaz's field. She hadn't just been happy because of the food. She'd been starting to plot. To plot a marriage between me, Ruth, and Boaz, one of the richest men in Bethlehem.

Only Naomi would dare to hope for such a thing.

Marriage to Boaz was of course the best possible thing that could happen to Naomi and me. In a way, I was surprised I hadn't thought of it myself. If I married Boaz, then *both* Naomi and I would go to live with him. I wouldn't be abandoning her because I would be staying in the same family—it would be almost like I was marrying Naomi's own son. So we'd *both* be cared for. There'd be no more back-breaking gleaning. At last we would have a chance to rest.

But… really?

Boaz is rich, I told myself. *He's an important man in Bethlehem. He won't want to take on a couple of poverty-stricken widows, one of whom isn't even an Israelite.*

But Boaz is rich, I counter-argued. *If anyone can afford to add two widows to his household, it's him.*

But he won't want to marry you, the first half of myself said. *You're a Moabite.*

But wouldn't you like to marry him? the second half of me responded. *Wouldn't you like to be married to a man like that?*

I admitted to myself that I would.

"Do you really think he'd say yes?" I whispered.

Naomi narrowed her eyes and looked me up and down, suddenly critical. "Well, he *might.* But we will need to make you a *lot* more presentable before we try it."

It turned out that there was no time like the present.

"Tonight, he will be at the threshing-floor," Naomi said. "You'll be able to get him alone. And the harvest is over, so he'll be in a good mood. Tonight is the night."

So for the next several hours, we got me ready. I scrubbed and scrubbed my whole body, removing every last speck of dirt from my skin. (This took a long time. There was a lot of dirt.)

Then I washed my hair, combing and combing it using the old wooden comb I'd had as a wedding gift from my mother years ago. I rubbed a little oil into my hair to make it shine, doing the same to my skin where it was dry and flaky. The oil was slightly perfumed—again, it had been a wedding gift. I hesitated over finishing the tiny pot, but Naomi insisted. This was our one chance, and we'd better give it all we had.

Once I'd selected my least patched dress and wound my nicest scarf around my waist as a sash, I sat on my bedroll and let Naomi comb my hair out one more time. She tied it back in a simple knot, then laid her own best headscarf over the top, being careful not to dislodge any strands of hair. Finally her hands touched my shoulders affectionately. "You're ready."

I let out a shuddering breath. "Are you sure about this? Going down to the threshing-floor on my own, when it's nearly dark? Isn't it a bit… dangerous?"

"I'm sure," Naomi answered firmly. "This is our best chance. Just stick to the plan."

I pulled an image of Boaz into my head to try to calm myself. Boaz, smiling out of his eyes. Boaz, saying that he understood my distress. Boaz, saying that he admired me. Boaz, saying that I had come under the Lord's wings for refuge.

Going out on my own after dark *was* dangerous—but surely with Boaz I would be safe.

So I nodded, stood up, and kissed Naomi on the cheek. "I'll do what you say," I told her. And I hurried to the door before I could change my mind.

The first part of the plan was to avoid being recognised. My approach to Boaz needed to be made in secret. But that was easier said than done when today was the last day of the harvest and the threshing-floors would be crowded with people.

All of Boaz's male servants and relatives would be there—not just the ones from the harvest-field but others too, the ones who cared for his animals and served in his home. I guessed there'd be at least a dozen men there, if not more. Plus, the point of threshing-floors was that they were open, flat places: that way, the wind could carry away the light husks and stalks after the heavier grain had been beaten out of them. Open and flat: there would not be a lot of hiding places.

Carefully I wrapped Naomi's scarf around my head and face, so that just my eyes could be seen. A breeze was picking up, and the ends of the fabric flapped behind me as I walked.

I heard the clip-clop of hooves coming towards me along the stony path. Instinctively I ducked into the shadows beneath an almond tree. There were two oxen coming; I smelled them before I saw them. A single servant led them, and two boys followed behind, carrying switches to whip the cows into action.

As the animals passed, I saw that there were bits of straw stuck to their sweating hides. They must have been used for the threshing. It was much easier to get oxen to trample the grain than it was to thresh it all by hand. And they were obviously on their way home. Which must mean that the evening's work was almost over. Good. As soon as they'd passed, I hurried back onto the path and onwards.

Now I was nearing the threshing floor. I could hear the familiar *thu-thud, thu-thud* of men beating grain. Lanterns had been lit, although it wasn't quite dark yet. And the men sang as they worked, their deep voices booming through the wind.

The Lord's inheritance is his people,
  The line of Israel is his portion.
In a desert land God found his child,
  In a barren, howling waste.
Then he shielded and sustained him,
  Kept him as the apple of his eye.

Listen, you heavens, and I will speak,
  Hear, you earth, the words I say.
I will proclaim the name of the Lord.
  Praise the greatness of our God!

Like an eagle that stirs up its nest
  And hovers over its young,
Like an eagle which spreads its wings
  And carries its chicks,
The Lord alone led Israel,
  No foreign god was with him.

Listen, you heavens, and I will speak,
  Hear, you earth, the words I say.
I will proclaim the name of the Lord.
  Praise the greatness of our God!

A shiver went through my spine as I listened. But I couldn't just stand there. I was only twenty paces away from the threshing-floor.

I looked around quickly. On the other side of the floor was a shrub, a spiky thing that didn't have many leaves yet. It wasn't a great hiding place, but it looked like my only option.

The men were all focused on the barley and the song. I ran around the edge of the threshing-floor, keeping my eyes fixed on the ground, my heart beating fast. I reached the bush and crouched behind it.

I let out a long breath.

Now it was time to wait.

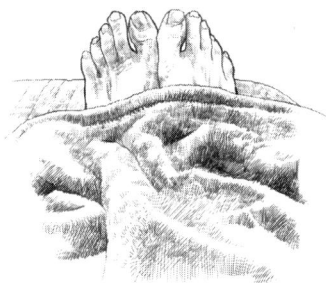

CHAPTER 21

A Long Night

It didn't take long for me to wish I hadn't chosen this bush to hide behind. It was dark now, and I had been crouching there for at least an hour. *Crouching* being the important word: I didn't want to ruin my clothes by sitting in the dirt. So I crouched. My leg muscles were fairly strong, but right now they were on fire.

The men had finished their threshing not long after I'd arrived, but it turned out the evening wasn't over: there was feasting to do. The singing carried on, but now it was punctuated by the chink of cups and the sound of appreciative chewing. Occasionally they stopped singing and talked in low, cheerful voices, but then someone always broke into song again.

All the while I crouched there, waiting.

Eventually they began to yawn and say it was time to sleep. I raised myself up very slightly to get a better view of the threshing-floor, which now had a complete circle of lanterns all around the edge. The threshed grain had been raked into a neat pile at one side, while all the unthreshed sheaves remained stacked at the other. In the swept middle part, the men lay down one by one.

I kept my eyes on Boaz. Despite the darkness, he was easy to recognise by the broad slope of his shoulders and the reddish glint of his beard. His sleeping spot was right by the grain pile, slightly apart from the rest of the men. He stood there, taking off his belt and his boots, and for a moment he looked just like a little boy getting ready for bed. Then I saw the flash of metal as he took his knife from his belt and hefted it in his hand. He'd sleep with it close by. Not so childlike, then.

Once he'd lain down, I could no longer see him—the grain pile was in the way. But I kept my gaze fixed on that spot even after the last lantern had been snuffed out, so I'd be sure to know where to go.

I gritted my teeth.

"Wait until he's fallen asleep," Naomi had said. "Then uncover his feet and lie down."

"What?!" I had said. "Uncover his feet?! Why?"

But now that I was here, I saw that it made sense. This needed to be done secretly, which meant waiting until the men were all asleep. But I couldn't go and shake Boaz awake or call his name. If I called out, I'd wake everyone. If I shook him, he'd spring on me with that knife before he'd even fully woken.

So instead I would obey Naomi and uncover his feet. Gradually, as the night wore on, he'd get cold. *That* would wake him up quietly.

I hoped.

Silence settled. One or two of the men rolled over in their sleep, but that was the only noise. The threshing-floor could not be comfortable, but they had worked hard and eaten well; I guessed they'd sleep heavily.

Eventually I heard a few slow, quiet snores. It was time to make my move.

I got up painfully, massaging my calves to relieve the stiffness. After a moment's hesitation, I removed my sandals. Better to have dirty feet than to wake everybody up with too-loud footsteps. I gripped them in one hand and crept around the side of the spiky bush. Step by quiet step, I walked the ten or fifteen paces to the threshing-floor. It was very dark.

Here was the grain pile; I felt the hard seeds against my fingers and heard a hiss as a few of them cascaded downwards. I pulled back, not wanting to disturb the whole heap. I skirted around it, dropping to the ground and crawling, heedless now of my clothes. It wouldn't matter how well dressed I was if I ended up with Boaz's knife stuck in me.

Here he was. Silently I thanked the Lord that Boaz

had picked a spot a little apart from his servants, so I could be sure it was him. He had covered himself completely with the big woollen cloth I'd seen him wrap around himself as a coat sometimes. His breathing was slow and even.

There was no point in hesitating; I had to do it. I gripped the edge of the woollen cloth in my fingers, and carefully drew it up and back, letting it rest on his legs.

His feet twitched.

I froze for a moment, my hands hovering over the cloth, my breath sucked in. But Boaz just rolled over, leaving his feet still uncovered, and made a slight smacking noise with his lips.

I breathed.

Then, trembling, I curled up next to his feet. I tucked my hands under my armpits to keep them warm. And the waiting began again.

When the moment came, I wasn't scared. It happened like I was in a dream.

Boaz's sleeping body jerked suddenly, and his legs drew themselves in. Then all at once he was sitting up, his knife in his hand. He'd seen me.

"Who's that?" he cried hoarsely, jabbing forward into the darkness.

"It's Ruth, your servant," I answered, and without

waiting for him to respond I grabbed the woollen cloth he'd been sleeping under and pulled it off his body and onto mine, holding it close to my chest like a child's comfort blanket.

"Sir," I said, "spread your wings over me, for you are a redeemer of our family."

He stared.

By now the clouds had cleared a little and the night was not so dark. His face was crumpled from sleep. Mine—well, who knew what mine looked like?

He lowered the knife. I still gripped the cloak.

I was about to repeat my request—maybe I should ask him more plainly—but I didn't have to.

"Ruth," Boaz breathed at last. "Are you asking me to marry you?"

I made a noise which was intended as a "Yes" but actually came out more like a squeak.

Then Boaz looked away from me, staring into the darkness, staying very still. He was thinking. But I couldn't tell *what* he was thinking.

CHAPTER 22

Not as Simple as You Think

"Well," Boaz said at last. "First of all, you've been very brave, coming here in the night like this. Maybe foolish, but definitely brave."

He paused. "Secondly, and more importantly, you've been very kind. I already knew you'd been kind to your mother-in-law, but this is an even greater kindness, to come to me like this instead of running after younger men. You could leave Naomi's family and find a future of your own—I'm sure either Joram or Ozias would have you, if you wanted—but you won't. You're sticking by your husband's family."

There was silence while he shifted position to sit cross-legged, leaning forward and propping his chin on one hand. He sucked his teeth, thinking.

I gripped his woollen cloth even closer to my chest. I felt I ought to look away deferentially while he came to his decision, but I couldn't. I had to see his face, as best I could in the moonlight. I had to try to understand what was going on in his mind.

I must have looked terrified because, when Boaz focused his attention on me again, his eyes immediately melted into tenderness. "Don't be afraid," he said gently. "You don't need to be afraid. I will do what you ask. Everyone in Bethlehem knows your strength of character."

I let out another small, wordless noise, this time without intending it at all.

"However," Boaz went on, "it isn't quite as simple as you think. We can't just arrange this between the two of us."

I pursed my lips, instantly feeling rebellious. Who on earth did he have to ask? His mother? Someone else in his clan? Surely Boaz, of all people, could be in charge of his own decisions?

"It's true that I'm a redeemer of the clan to which we both belong," he explained. "But there is another redeemer, a man who's more closely related to Elimelek than I am. This man has a better right to redeem you than me."

I took this in.

Another redeemer. Another family member I didn't know about. A closer relative than Boaz.

I wanted to say, *You're the one I've come to. You're the one I'm safe with. Can't we just pretend this other person doesn't exist?*

But if there was one thing I knew about Boaz, it was that he was a fair and generous man. There was no way on earth he'd avoid doing what was correct in this situation. And what was correct was offering me to this other person, this other relative. Giving him, whoever he was, the opportunity to marry me.

Boaz was looking around at the dark threshing-floor, musing. "All right," he said at last. "Here's what I think. First, you should stay here for the night. It's not safe to go all the way back to town, not until it's light. But you must leave early, before the men wake. Nobody must know that a woman came to the threshing-floor."

He nodded, approving of his own plan. "In the morning, we'll see if the other redeemer wants to do his duty. If he does, good; he can redeem you. But if he is not willing, I swear to you, as surely as the Lord lives, I will do it."

And that was that. There was nothing to do but lie down again and try to sleep.

"Ruth," came Boaz's whisper as the first pale light of morning made its way across the threshing-floor. I had been watching it for some time, admiring how the first rays of the sun caressed each sleeping form. The sky was still a deep blue, but it was tinged pink like cherry blossom.

I was warm under Boaz's blanket, and frankly I didn't want to get up. But the sun would rise soon, and before long its heat would be fierce. There was no escaping the day.

"Ruth!" A louder whisper this time.

I uncurled myself.

Boaz was smiling broadly. Excitedly, even. "You must go home," he whispered. "But first, look, come here… Bring that shawl you're wearing and hold it out."

Wearily I stood up, letting the big woollen cloth fall to the floor. I took the shawl that I'd tied around my waist and held it out listlessly, not really understanding Boaz's purpose.

Then I saw what he was going to do. He was waving a large wooden scoop, which he was about to dig into the heap of barley.

He was going to fill up my shawl with grain.

"I don't want you to go back to your mother-in-law empty-handed," he whispered enthusiastically as he drew the scoop out of the pile, full. "Look—are you ready?"

Hurriedly I twisted the ends of the scarf in my hands to form stronger handles, and let the centre of the fabric hang loose in the middle. He poured the grain from the scoop into it and then whispered, "Another!"

I was amazed. Gone was the serious Boaz of the middle of the night. Now he had such a twinkle in his eye, I felt like we were best friends who'd known each other all our lives, doing something naughty together. But of course Boaz *owned* this grain; it was his to do with as he liked.

And now it was mine. He gave me six huge scoops— he would've given more, I suspect, if I'd been able to carry it. As it was, I staggered under the awkward load. Looking apologetic, Boaz helped me tie the ends of the scarf together to make a bundle, then beamed at me in triumph.

I met his gaze just for a moment—then quickly looked away. There might not be any more moments like this. Not if the other redeemer wanted to marry me.

"I'd better go," I said stiffly.

Boaz faltered. "Ah… yes. Good."

I looked around for my sandals, handing him the bundle while I put them on. I gave a low bow, avoiding eye contact. Then I took the bundle again and tiptoed towards Bethlehem.

CHAPTER 23

The Man in the Cap

Naomi received the huge bundle of barley like it had been owed to her all along, and generally looked very smug. She seemed to think it was entirely good news.

"Just wait, my daughter," she said with perfect assurance. "The man won't rest until the matter is settled today." Then she settled herself on her bedroll and went back to sleep.

But I couldn't sleep. And I didn't much want to wait, either. I'd waited all night. I'd had enough of waiting. I knew where Boaz would go to speak to this other redeemer: the town gate, where all important business was decided. And I was determined to witness their conversation for myself.

I ate some food and drank some water. I changed into my oldest work dress and wrapped my shabbiest headscarf around my face. And I went out again into the streets of Bethlehem.

The whole area by the gate was covered with fallen blossom from the big acacia tree. It was as if it had been purposely decorated for a wedding. I picked up a yellow flower and twizzled it in my fingers as I looked around for a spot where I could sit—sit, not crouch—and remain inconspicuous.

There: a little way along from the gate, a stone jutted out of the wall. I perched on it nervously, looking at the ground so that I wouldn't meet anyone's eyes.

The gate was the one point of entry into the walled town, as well as being the place where the elders sat and business was conducted. So it was busy. Hooves of goats and cattle clopped past; gossiping neighbours went by, and harvesters holding flails. I thought I heard the piercing voice of Melchi, the woman I'd met on my first day in Ephrathah, and stole a glance up to be sure it was her. Yes. She was speaking with another woman—something about the price of wool. Other discussions were happening all around the acacia tree; I let the voices wash over me, half listening, waiting until I heard the one voice I really cared about.

Then, there he was.

He came in through the gate with two servants behind him and sat on one of the stumps by the tree. He looked big and impressive, with his woollen cloak wrapped around him and his belt fastened on top.

"Boaz," said a voice, sounding surprised. "I thought you'd be threshing all day today."

"I have some business to settle first," Boaz replied calmly.

I kept my eyes fixed on the yellow flower in my hands. It was battered already from the twizzling; now I dug a fingernail into it, cutting one of the petals in two, and then another.

"Boaz," another voice said: one of the elders, I thought, coming to take his place by the gate for the day. "The Lord be with you."

"The Lord bless you," Boaz replied. Then there was a sudden rustle as some more footsteps clicked past. "Friend! Friend!" cried Boaz. "I'd like to speak with you. Come here, sit down."

I risked another glance in their direction.

Boaz was taking a cup from one of his servants and pouring a little wine into it from a skin.

He offered it to the man who was now coming over to sit beside him.

The other redeemer.

The man was tall, thin, and had an embroidered cap covering his grey hair. He took the wine appreciatively and spread himself across the stump that neighboured Boaz's.

That was when I saw his face.

It was the same man I had seen on two occasions before: first on the day of our arrival in Bethlehem and then on the second day of the harvest. This was the man who had stared at us with such cold curiosity.

Now I understood why. *He* was the other redeemer. He was the man who should have been helping us this entire time.

And, he was the man who might be about to agree to marry me. And if he did, I wouldn't have a choice, not really. It'd be him or poverty.

To stop myself from shaking, I bent to pick up another flower, then started crushing it savagely between my fingers.

Now Boaz was beckoning to the other elders who were sitting or standing around the acacia tree. There were ten of them, all men with grey or white hair and well-made clothes. Men respected for their wisdom, or perhaps their wealth. One by one they sat down around Boaz and the other redeemer, forming a circle.

I pulled my headscarf back a little so that my ears were free. I wanted to hear all of this.

Boaz was smiling all around him. He made a sign to his servants, who produced more cups and more wine, and handed them out to the assembled elders.

"What's this about?" asked the other redeemer impatiently.

But Boaz only smiled again, pointing out the servants as if to say, *Wait till everyone's had their wine.*

A crowd was beginning to form; people wanted to know what was going on. The whole area under the acacia tree was still and quiet, waiting for Boaz to speak.

Finally he cleared his throat.

"Naomi, who has come back from Moab, is selling the piece of land that belonged to our relative Elimelek," he said to the other redeemer. "I thought that I should bring the matter to your attention and suggest that you buy it, in the presence of those seated here and in the presence of the elders of my people."

Boaz glanced around the circle, nodding at all the elders, then looked back at the man beside him. "If you will redeem it, do so. But if you will not, let me know, and I will redeem it. You have the best right to do it, but I am next in line."

I hadn't expected this. The field? Why was Boaz talking about the field?

The other redeemer was nodding slowly. "I've heard of this. Yes, I will redeem it. Why not?"

Then Boaz flexed his fingers. "There is one complication."

"Oh?"

"As you know," said Boaz, "it is the law among our people that when a man dies leaving no son to inherit his property, and if his widow is still young, she is taken as a wife by another member of the family. If the Lord enables her to bear a child by her new husband, this son becomes the heir to the dead man's property. In this way, the family line is guaranteed, and the clan is strengthened."

This was news to me. If I had a son, he'd inherit Mahlon's property? He'd inherit the field? Was that what Boaz was saying?

"In this case," Boaz went on, "the field of Elimelek was inherited on his death by his eldest son Mahlon, who himself sadly died without an heir. This is why the property needs to be redeemed. However, Mahlon did leave a widow. A young woman who is still of marriageable age."

Boaz looked around the circle again. "With the elders' approval, I propose that on the day you buy the land from Naomi, you will also marry Ruth the Moabite, the dead man's widow. This way, the dead man's name stays with his property. If Ruth has a son, he will inherit both Mahlon's name and his field."

My heart raced as I thought this through, trying to catch up.

If I had a son, then the field would go to him. That meant that my new husband would buy it, but... but he'd have to pass it on as soon as my son came of age.

My new husband would spend his money on it, but it would never really be his.

This was why Boaz was tying the field and the marriage together. It had to be. Buying the field in combination with marrying me was a bad use of money.

Boaz wanted to show that it was a bad deal. He wanted the other redeemer to say no. He wanted to take the deal himself, even though it would cost him.

Boaz actually *wanted* me to be his wife.

I realised that the other redeemer was speaking. His lips were curled into a sneer. "Ruth the Moabite?" he spat. "Why on earth would I want a Moabite as my wife? She has nothing to offer me. Nothing that's worthwhile."

Boaz's voice was quiet and calm as he answered. "She offers her faith. Her loyalty to her husband's family, and to her mother-in-law, and to the Lord."

I felt the very tips of my ears go pink. I couldn't help but look at Boaz. And as I did, he met my gaze—calmly, as if he'd known I was there all along.

He winked.

Then he turned back to the other redeemer with a polite smile.

The other redeemer looked disgusted. "Then I cannot redeem the field," he said bluntly. "I don't wish to marry the Moabite girl. You redeem the field yourself. I can't."

Every eye in the hushed crowd swivelled towards Boaz.

"Good," he said. "Then, with the approval of the elders…?"

The white-haired men leaned towards each other to discuss it. Boaz beamed broadly around as they did so. Finally the oldest elder, a man with a long white beard and a walking stick, gave him a nod.

With a scowl, the other redeemer reached down and untied one of his sandals. He thumped it into Boaz's hand. "The agreement is made. I resign my right to redeem the field. Buy it yourself."

Then Boaz stood up and looked around at the whole crowd of Ephrathites assembled in front of him.

"Today," he declared in a booming voice, "you are witnesses that I have bought from Naomi all the property of Elimelek, Kilion and Mahlon. I have also acquired Ruth the Moabite, Mahlon's widow, as my wife. This way, the dead man's name will stay with his property and not disappear from among his family or from his hometown. Today you are witnesses!"

"We are witnesses," they chorused.

One of the elders stood up. "May the Lord make the woman who is coming into your home like Rachel and Leah, who together built up the family of Israel," he said. "May you have standing in Ephrathah. May you be famous in Bethlehem!"

Boaz bowed deeply to the crowd. Then he turned around, looked straight at me, and broke into the most enormous smile.

CHAPTER 24

Another Story

Before I finish my story, my little love, I want to remind you of another story: the story of Israel.

A very long time ago, the Lord God said to Abraham, "Leave your country, your people and your father's household, and go to the land I will show you. I will make you into a great nation, and I will bless you; and all peoples on earth will be blessed through you."

So Abraham went, as the Lord had told him. He travelled to the land that God told him to go to and pitched his tent underneath a spreading tree.

Then the Lord appeared to him and said, "I will give this land to your descendants." But Abraham and his wife Sarah had no children. Who was going to continue their family line and inherit the land God had promised? It seemed it would have to be Abraham's servant. Abraham said to the Lord (without wishing to sound too much like he was complaining), "You've given me no children."

But in time God did give him a child. He enabled Sarah to bear a son, and this son was named Isaac. And God said, "I will give the land to Isaac's descendants."

When Abraham's son Isaac was grown, the Lord provided him with a wife and children. And when Isaac's son Jacob was grown, God did the same.

Jacob, in fact, had twelve sons, plus a daughter. And each of them had sons. In each generation, the Lord God was the one who strengthened the family line. He provided wives, and he provided children. At every moment when it seemed like the family might not survive, the Lord saved it. The descendants of Abraham multiplied until they became a whole nation: the Israelites.

But the Israelites lived far away from the land God had promised. In fact, they were in Egypt, where they were trapped as slaves.

By this point in the story, however, it's obvious that God was not going to leave them there. These were his people, whom he loved. And he is a kind God. He said to them, "I am the Lord. I will redeem you. I will take you as my own people, and I will be your God."

So he freed them from slavery. The descendants of Abraham, Isaac and Jacob left the land of Egypt which they knew, and went to the land God had promised to give them, which they had never been to before.

God gave each tribe and each family its own patch of the land. One patch was a town called Bethlehem

Ephrathah. There, in time, lived the grandparents of Elimelek, of Naomi, and of Boaz.

The eldest son of Elimelek was Mahlon, and Mahlon married a Moabite whose name was Ruth (that's me!). But Mahlon and Ruth had no children, and Mahlon died. Once again the family line seemed to have reached its end.

But the Lord is a redeemer.

Ruth the Moabite left her country, her people, and her mother's house, and came to the land God had promised his people—a land she hadn't known before. She married Boaz, another member of her husband's clan. And the Lord, in his kindness, enabled Ruth to bear a son, whose name was Obed. He was Boaz's son, but he was also Mahlon's son. And so the family line continued.

Obed, sweet boy, do you understand? Do you understand who you are?

When you were born, Boaz wrapped you up with his own hands in a yellow blanket. I was very tired and I needed to sleep, so he took you and put you in Naomi's arms. She was sitting just beside my bed. Her hair was all grey and her skin was as wrinkled as prunes, but when she held you that first time, she looked like a young woman who'd just got married. Like someone who'd found a whole new kind of rest. Her smile was soft and a little bit wobbly.

Then the door burst open and others came into the room—Iscah and Ahinoam and the serving-women of the household. They'd all been waiting anxiously outside. Immediately they gathered around Naomi and started cooing over you. Your eyes, your nose, your little hands, your swirl of dark hair flattened against your soft scalp… An argument started about whether you looked more like me or more like Boaz.

But Iscah came to the other side of the bed. She squeezed my hand and asked if I needed anything.

"Sleep," I said.

Iscah grinned. "We'll get them all out of here in a moment, I promise."

Then she looked over at Naomi, who still had you in her arms—there was no chance she was going to let anyone else cuddle you yet. She was looking into your face, holding you tight, smiling that wobbly smile.

"Look," Iscah said softly. "A son has been born to Naomi."

And it was true.

Do you know, Obed, that you are a redeemer? It's your job to look after Naomi in her old age. You're her grandson, her big hope and joy. And if any other member of the family falls on hard times, it'll be your job to help them too.

Maybe you'll even be like your father, Boaz. Maybe

you'll take pity on someone like me one day. An outsider—someone who doesn't belong in the family of Israel, not by rights. And you'll bring them in.

Ahinoam had heard what Iscah said. She smirked. "It seems to me, Naomi, that Ruth is better to you than *seven* sons would be."

Then Naomi looked at me, lying there on the bed in our home in Bethlehem. And for once, she didn't purse her lips.

Epilogue

So Boaz married Ruth, and they had a son, and their son's name was Obed.

Obed's son was Jesse, and Jesse's son was David, and David became the ruler of all Israel.

After that, the family line went on, just as it always had. There were good kings and bad kings. There were battles and disasters. Children were born and crops were grown. Through it all, of course, God remained faithful.

Until, hundreds and hundreds of years after the time of Ruth, a crowd of shepherds were sitting in one of the fields around Bethlehem…

It was dark, and they were huddled down under piles of cloaks, trying to stay awake. There was silence, apart from the occasional stirring of sheep. Someone had just thrown another log on the sputtering fire, and the shepherds' eyes watched the lazy sparks float up and away.

Then the whole sky lit up.

The shepherds almost jumped out of their skins. Their stiff old coats fell off their shoulders. One tattered sheepskin only just missed the fire as it fell to the ground, but the shepherds didn't notice.

There was an angel!

He was shining. They couldn't look at him properly. They covered their faces, afraid they'd end up blind. Or dead.

But the angel told them not to be scared.

"Today in the town of David," he said, "a Saviour has been born to you; he is the Messiah, the Lord."

Now the shepherds' white eyes stared out of their grimy faces. Their fear was replaced by astonishment. The town of David? That meant Bethlehem—their own city. The town just the other side of the hill. The town they'd all been born in.

And today a Saviour had been born *there*… and born *for them*?

How could God be so *kind*?!

But it was true. A Saviour *had* been born. His name was Jesus.

The story of Jesus might seem very different to the story of Ruth, but the truth is that you can't have one without the other. That's partly because Jesus was born into the family of Ruth—it was generations later, but you can trace the family line all the way from her to him. But it's also because Jesus is a redeemer.

Jesus was born to save people. Not just to look after them in their old age, but to look after them *for ever*. Not just to make them part of his family, but to make them part of *God's* family.

This is true even for outsiders. Jesus invites us in, whoever we are and wherever we live and whatever our background. To redeem us, he didn't just buy a field; the cost he paid was to die on a cross. Because he did that, anyone who puts their trust in him can be part of God's family for ever. Safe. Home. Loved. Accepted.

If you thought that Boaz was kind, and if you thought that Ruth was loyal, here is someone who is even more of both those things. There is no end to his kindness and no limit to his loyalty.

No wonder the shepherds were so excited to hear the news!

Breathlessly, the men looked at each other. The angel had left, and the light had gone. But even in the gloom, they could see in each other's faces that it hadn't been a dream.

"Let's go to Bethlehem," someone said.

"Let's go *now*!" agreed another.

They found the baby lying in a manger. As they looked at him, they knew that it was really true. God really *is* kind. A redeemer had been born for *them*!

Notes

The story of Ruth is told in just four chapters of the Bible—you can read it pretty quickly! In my retelling, I've added all sorts of details along the way. So, in this section, I've explained the thinking behind what I've written.

This retelling is an attempt to bring the Bible story to life in a faithful and accurate way. But it's only my version!

A NOTE ON GOD'S PEOPLE

In Old Testament times, God's people were known as the Israelites—so the land they lived in was known as Israel. The Old Testament Israelites were a people group that God had chosen, and he had a plan to bless the world through them. The New Testament part of the Bible makes it clear that this plan was fulfilled in Jesus. He was an Israelite (although by then, Israelites were known as Jews) who lived in what we now call the 1st century AD. Jesus' life, death and resurrection were the way that God kept his promises to his people. And now, through faith in Jesus, anyone can become part of God's people—it isn't about who you are, where you come from, or where you live. It's just about making Jesus your King.

As you'll discover, the story of Ruth is very much a part of God's big plan to bring outsiders into his people.

A NOTE ON KINDNESS
The words "kind" and "kindness" pop up a lot in my retelling. They also appear several times in the original book of Ruth.

In English, we use the word "kind" to mean "nice"— you are being kind when you help someone out in a small way. But in the Bible, it's a much bigger, deeper word than that. This same word in Hebrew is often used to describe God's kindness and love towards his people (for example, in Genesis 39:21 and Exodus 34:6, where it's translated as "love"). And God doesn't just do good deeds for his people; he never gives up on them! So when you see the word "kind" or "kindness" in this book, you shouldn't just think "nice"—you should think "deep, never-giving-up love".

CHAPTER ONE
The first scene in this chapter is taken from Ruth 1:6-18. But it's just a taster for now—we'll come back to it later!

There's a lot in these first six chapters that I had to invent. Ruth and Orpah were real people, but everything else about their families and village is made up, based on what we know about what life was like in those times.

In the book of Ruth, we only meet Ruth as an adult. But we know that Naomi and her family stayed in Moab for a total of ten years. At some point in that time (spoiler alert!), Ruth gets married—we don't know when exactly. So I've imagined that the Israelites first arrived when Ruth was twelve; several years will pass before Ruth gets married, and then several more years before the scene at the start of chapter 1 of this book.

CHAPTER TWO

"Ephrathah" was another name for the town of Bethlehem. (Originally it may have been the name of a village near Bethlehem.) So, if someone was an Ephrathite, it meant they came from Bethlehem.

The Moabites lived on the eastern side of the Dead Sea. Several conflicts between Moabites and Israelites happened in the same approximate time period as the story of Ruth. However, these are not mentioned in the book of Ruth, so I've assumed that the story took place during a time of peace. Even so, it's clear that in general, Israelites and Moabites did not get on at all!

CHAPTER THREE

The events of this chapter are entirely invented. I thought it was important to show something about Moabite religion, and how it was different to the Israelites' beliefs.

We know that the Moabites worshipped the god Chemosh, but since people in those times generally worshipped lots of gods, I've described several here. It might seem strange to worship a stone, but this really happened in the ancient world. Most often, people used human-made figurines to represent their gods, but there's also lots of evidence for uncarved stones being used. Some of them were probably meteorites (which is why Dinah says that the stone in her shrine fell from the sky).

The Bible is clear that the God of Israel is the only real God, and only he should be worshipped (Exodus 20:2-3; Deuteronomy 4:39). But even some Israelites might have believed that other "gods" existed—they might just have thought they were less powerful than their own God.

CHAPTER FOUR

You can read more about gleaning in Leviticus 19:9-10 and 23:22, and Deuteronomy 24:19. This practice wasn't just a custom—it was a law that was given by God. It's really striking that the last bits of food in the field or on the trees were not just left for the poor but also for foreigners. God had chosen the Israelites as his own people, but that never meant that he didn't care about other people as well.

CHAPTER FIVE

The Bible doesn't tell us much about Elimelek's death. Ruth 1:3 simply says, "Now Elimelek, Naomi's husband, died, and she was left with her two sons."

The scene with Zowelah is invented. Actually, the whole character of Zowelah is invented! Her character helps us understand why it was so tough to be a widow in the ancient world, especially one without a son. (This will be important later on.) Nowadays it's no problem to be an unmarried woman: many women never get married in the first place, and becoming widowed, while very sad, is manageable. But in ancient times, being a widow was a disaster. You needed a man's strength and protection for all sorts of things, and without it, you struggled. That's why God often instructed his people to take care of widows. They needed help!

You can read about the story of Abraham's call in Genesis 12:1-7. (He's called Abram in that passage—his name changed later.) You can also read God's promises to Abraham and to his grandson Jacob in Genesis 17:1-8 and 28:10-15.

In this chapter, Naomi refers to God as "the Lord". He is often called this in the Bible and the word appears in capitals—Lord. It's a way of showing respect for God. Even his name is holy, so Israelites avoided using it and instead called him "Adonai", "the Lord".

CHAPTER SIX

A lot of time passes in this chapter. Ruth 1:5 very briefly tells us about the death of Mahlon and Kilion. The focus there isn't on Ruth's grief but on Naomi's: she "was left without her two sons and her husband". In a world where women needed the protection of a man, this was a very serious situation indeed.

CHAPTER SEVEN

You can read the original version of the scene with Naomi, Orpah and Ruth in Ruth 1:8-18. I wonder whether you agree with the way I've imagined it—do you think I've got everyone's motives and feelings right?

Ruth's decision to go with Naomi is astonishing. It really doesn't make much sense! Ruth will have a much better chance of a successful future if she stays in Moab and marries again there. There's also the issue of Ruth being a Moabite—she's unlikely to receive a warm welcome in Israel. Yet Ruth, unlike Orpah, chooses to follow Naomi. And not just that—she makes this amazing promise to be loyal to her for the rest of her life. This would be a very unusual thing to do in today's world, let alone in a time when women really needed to prioritise marriage and children.

CHAPTER EIGHT

You can read the story of Jacob and Esau starting in Genesis 25:21. The bit about Jacob meeting Rachel is in Genesis 29. The story of Rachel's death is in Genesis 35:16-20.

Genesis 26:35 says that Esau's two wives were "a source of grief" to his parents. This is part of a pattern in the Old Testament: if you marry someone from outside of the people of Israel—someone who doesn't know and worship the God of Israel—it tends to go badly.

The law about marriage which Naomi explains to Ruth is described in Deuteronomy 25:5-10.

CHAPTER NINE

Ruth 1:1 tells us that the story took place "in the days when the judges ruled". This was the period in Israel's history after they had settled in the land God had promised them, but before they got their first king. It was a very unstable and often violent time. The people were led by judges who were chosen by God, but these judges had limited power, and there were times of real chaos and conflict alongside times of peace. The Bible tells us that in this period "all the people did whatever seemed right in their own eyes" (Judges 21:25, NLT); in other words, many people did not worship and obey God. This is why I've portrayed Bethlehem as a place where some people follow God and obey his laws, but many don't. There is lots of invented detail in this chapter, but it all contributes to that portrayal.

The other thing I wanted to show in this chapter was the fact that Bethlehem was ruled over by elders. This was a group of older men who were responsible for making decisions about who was right and wrong, and for witnessing legal transactions—a bit like court judges today.

CHAPTER TEN

You can read about Naomi and Ruth's arrival in Bethlehem in Ruth 1:19-22.

It isn't a coincidence that the woman calls Naomi "sweet". That's actually what the name Naomi means. So what Naomi actually said was, "Don't call me

Naomi". And she told the woman to call her "Mara", which means "bitter" (the opposite of sweet). Naomi isn't only saying that the Lord has made her life bitter—she's saying that she herself is bitter. It's like her previous self has gone, and she feels like a new, more unpleasant person.

CHAPTER ELEVEN

The details in this chapter are invented. I am picking up on the fact that all the way through the story in the Bible, Ruth is called "Ruth the Moabite" or just "the Moabite". This was not meant as a compliment!

CHAPTER TWELVE

The events of this chapter are taken from Ruth 2:1-3.

Ruth wasn't very safe, being out on her own like this. Remember that many Israelites at this time were not obeying God. It's clear that, without the protection of a husband or father, Ruth was very vulnerable.

The fields in Ruth's time would have been much smaller than they tend to be today. Most people, if not everyone, would have been farming their own crops. And they had no machinery to help them. They used sickles, which were basically big hook-shaped knives.

We are not told that Ruth prayed for God's help here. But I think that we are meant to realise that God was helping her—so I wanted to make that clear.

CHAPTER THIRTEEN

The events of this chapter are taken from Ruth 2:4-13.

CHAPTER FOURTEEN

The events of this chapter are taken from Ruth 2:14-18.

We don't learn the names of any of Boaz's workers in the Bible. Iscah, and the other workers who you'll meet later on, are invented.

CHAPTER FIFTEEN

The events of this chapter are taken from Ruth 2:19-22. I invented the part about the potter's wife accusing Ruth of thievery, and we don't know where Ruth and Naomi were staying. But the accusation does seem likely! Ruth 2:17 tells us that she has gathered a whole ephah of grain. An ephah is an ancient measurement—it was about ten days' worth of food. Imagine it—all of the food you would eat for a whole ten days, all in one bundle! That's a lot, given that Ruth is supposed to be just picking up bits and pieces that have been dropped accidentally.

CHAPTER SIXTEEN

This chapter is largely invented. Ruth 2:23 tells us that "Ruth stayed close to the women of Boaz to glean until the barley and what harvests were finished"—that's seven weeks of the barley harvest, followed by seven weeks of the wheat harvest. So I have imagined some things that happened during that time.

CHAPTER SEVENTEEN

Here are some of God's laws about widows, orphans and foreigners:

- Love foreigners as yourself (Leviticus 19: 33-34).
- Help those who become poor (Leviticus 25:35) and don't make them work as slaves (v 39).
- Set aside money and food and give it to "the Levites [the priests] (who have no land allotted to them or any inheritance of their own) and the foreigners, the fatherless and the widows" (Deuteronomy 14:28-29).
- Give generously to the poor and needy, and every seventh year you must cancel everything they owe you (Deuteronomy 15:1-11).

These laws were specifically for the nation of Israel in Bible times. Christians don't obey them in the same way today. However, Christians are called to be generous and to look after those who are needy or vulnerable (see, for example, Luke 12:33; 1 Timothy 6:18; James 1:27).

CHAPTER EIGHTEEN

At this point in the history of God's people, the land that belonged to each family was hugely important. It wasn't just how you made your living; it was also a big part of your connection to the Lord. After all, this was the land that God had promised to his people, and God had given specific instructions about which parts of it were to belong to whom. So, it was important that every family kept their land. You were allowed to sell it, but it was never sold permanently—it always eventually belonged to your family again. (You can read about this in Leviticus 25:8-24.) This was all supposed to be a reminder that, actually, the land belonged to God first and foremost (Leviticus 25:23). Everything that the Israelites had came directly from him.

CHAPTER NINETEEN

Boaz mentions a prayer that is prayed in Israel when a couple gets married. This is half-invented. We will meet this prayer later in the story, but we don't know that it was regularly recited at weddings.

What does it mean for God to bless the family or the people through someone? Well, this is partly about being someone who walks in God's ways. If you are loyal and kind, a peacemaker, and a hard worker, you will naturally improve the lives of those around you. But in the context of the Old Testament, it's also about something more specific. As the Old Testament traces the story of the family of Abraham and Sarah, there are repeated promises about the future of that family. For example, God said about Sarah, "Kings of peoples will come from her" (Genesis 17:15-16). Later, God said to King David, "I will raise up your offspring to succeed you, your own flesh and blood, and I will establish his kingdom" (2 Samuel 7:12). These promises all led towards Jesus, who would one day be born as part of the same family, and who is God's perfect King. We can all receive blessing through Jesus. And anyone in the Old Testament who was part of Jesus' family, stretching all the way back to Abraham, was part of the story of how we got that blessing.

CHAPTER TWENTY

You can read this part of the story in Ruth 3:1-4.

The strange thing about this story is that it doesn't quite fit the actual law about redeemers. Take a look at Leviticus 25:25-55, and you'll see that marriage wasn't part of what redeemers did. What seems to be happening is that the law about redeemers was being blended with the law about a man marrying his dead brother's widow (Deuteronomy 25:5-10)—that's why Naomi has had the idea of Boaz redeeming Ruth by marrying her.

The song in this chapter is based on Deuteronomy 32:1-3 and 9-12. It was sung when the Israelites came out of slavery in Egypt, and I've imagined that it was passed down through the generations. Perhaps you can spot some of the connections between this song and the main story.

CHAPTER TWENTY-ONE

You can read this part of the story in Ruth 3:7-9.

What did you think of the way Ruth proposed to Boaz? Generally, in ancient times, marriages were agreed between the men of the two families. So it's very unusual that Ruth makes a proposal herself.

But Ruth doesn't just say, "Will you marry me?" Instead she refers back to something that Boaz said previously. Back in 2:12 (and in chapter 13 of this book), Boaz said that Ruth had come under God's wings for refuge. It isn't a coincidence that now Ruth says, "Spread your wings over me". She is asking Boaz for protection—the kind of protection that the Lord gives.

In the NIV Bible translation, Ruth's proposal is translated as "Spread the corner of your garment over me". That's because the Hebrew word for "wing" was also used to mean the edge or corner of a piece of clothing. But I think Ruth used this word very deliberately, so I kept the word "wing", while also including a piece of clothing in the scene.

CHAPTER TWENTY-TWO
The events in this chapter are told in Ruth 3:10-15.

Boaz says to Ruth, "Everyone in Bethlehem knows your strength of character". This phrase "strength of character" gets translated differently in different Bible versions. In the NIV it's "You are a woman of noble character". The ESV, meanwhile, has "you are a worthy woman". But the most literal translation would be "you are a woman of strength" or "you are a powerful woman"! It's actually the same word that is used to describe Boaz in 2:1—there it's translated "a man of standing" or "a worthy man". I like the idea that Ruth and Boaz have the same strength. Boaz is important and rich—he's literally strong and powerful. Ruth is weaker, smaller and poorer. But both of them have the same strength inside.

CHAPTER TWENTY-THREE
Naomi's brief conversation with Ruth is told in Ruth 3:16-18. The scene at the gate is told in Ruth 4:1-12.

The other redeemer is introduced very suddenly in the Bible narrative, and we never even learn his name. But in my version, we've actually met him twice already. That's my invention.

The Bible doesn't tell us that Ruth was there at the gate when Boaz met with the other redeemer. But I decided to allow her to witness it, even though in real life she probably didn't!

In the Bible, the reason the other redeemer gives for not marrying Ruth is "I might endanger my own estate" (that is, his property). Bible experts disagree about what this means. I've taken the view that the man doesn't like the idea that his future son with Ruth would inherit the field he's buying.

CHAPTER TWENTY-FOUR

The book of Ruth doesn't mention a link with Abraham, but I was really struck by the similarities between Ruth and Abraham, so I really wanted to include this wider story at this point!

What the book of Ruth does include at the end is a genealogy—a kind of family tree (Ruth 4:18-22). While it doesn't start with Abraham, it is about Abraham's family. It starts with Perez, who was a grandson of Abraham's grandson Jacob. It turns out that Perez was the ancestor of Boaz. Then the genealogy continues: Boaz was the father of Obed, Obed was the father of Jesse, and Jesse was the father of David. You might know that David was the greatest king of Israel in the Old Testament—and he was descended from Ruth and Boaz! So this genealogy is a reminder that in the story of Ruth, God wasn't just providing for Ruth and Naomi; he was providing for his whole people.

He was also providing for you and me today. If you turn to Matthew 1, you'll find a longer version of the same genealogy—and this time it goes all the way to Jesus.

The other parts of this chapter are taken from Ruth 4:13-17.

EPILOGUE

Back in the final chapter, you read the words "A son has been born to Naomi". This is actually translated slightly differently in the NIV: "Naomi has a son" (Ruth 4:17). That's a bit strange, because Obed is Ruth's son, not Naomi's! But in the original Hebrew, it literally says something more like, "A son has been born to (or for) Naomi". Although Obed was Ruth's son, his birth was all about Naomi—all about looking after her and keeping her family line going. That's why Ruth 4:14 describes Obed as Naomi's redeemer.

We see the same wording in a couple of other places in the Bible: Isaiah 9:6 and Luke 2:11. Both are talking about the birth of Jesus. Isaiah 9:6 says, "To us a child is born, to us a son is given". Luke 2:11 says, "A Saviour has been born to you." So, there is a link here between the story of Ruth and the birth of Jesus—as I've tried to explain in this epilogue.

BOOK CLUB

DISCUSSION GUIDE

ON CHAPTERS 1–7

1. What did you think about how people in Moab responded to the Israelites at first? What did Ruth think of them, and how did her view change?

2. Why was worshipping God different to worshipping the Moabite "gods"?

3. Read Ruth 1:6-18. Why do you think Orpah stayed in Moab while Ruth left with Naomi? What would you have done?

4. What impression did you have of Naomi in these chapters? What was she like? Do you think you would have got on with her?

ON CHAPTERS 8-15

5. What was Bethlehem like when Ruth and Naomi arrived? Do you think it was what they were expecting?

6. What do you think it was like for Ruth to go out to the fields for the first time? How would you have been feeling if you were her?

7. What was Boaz like? Why do you think he was so kind to Ruth?

8. Read Ruth 2:11-12 and 19-20. What do Boaz and Naomi think about what God is like?

ON CHAPTERS 16-21

9. What do you think of God's commands about re- deemers? Do you think that was a good system?

10. Do you think you would have found it easy or hard to trust the Lord if you were Ruth in this part of the story?

11. What does the threshing-floor part of the story tell us about what Ruth was like?

12. Read Ruth 3:7-11. What did Boaz think about Ruth and why?

ON CHAPTERS 22-24 AND EPILOGUE

13. What are some reasons for Boaz not to marry Ruth? Why do you think he did it anyway?

14. Read Ruth 1:20-21 and 4:14-15. How did Naomi's relationship with God change throughout the story? Was she right or wrong about him at the beginning?

15. What similarities did you spot between Abraham and Ruth? What do their stories tell you about what it means to have faith?

16. What impression of God did you get throughout the story? How could that impact your own life?

17. What does it mean that Jesus is a redeemer? How does it make you feel about yourself and about him?

Acknowledgements

The story of Ruth was brought to life for me through a period of loneliness and a period of illness. Both times I found myself being blown away by more kindness than I expected or deserved! So, my thanks are due especially to Daf and Boo, Rachel, Catherine and Chris. Your kindness, and your willingness to invite me in, has given me a picture of the Lord's own extraordinary kindness, and helped me to feel his love.

As I wrote, I was also inspired by Sarah and Alison, two friends whom I enormously admire for their example of steadfast kindness and persevering faith in the face of suffering and loss. I thank the Lord for his work in you.

Thanks to Steph and Matt for your unending enthusiasm and encouragement. Thanks to Carl, Jeab, Geoff and many other colleagues at The Good Book Company for your belief in my writing and in me generally. Thanks to Rachel (again) for your interest, help, wisdom and friendship as I wrote and edited this book. Finally, thanks to André Parker, Alex Webb-Peploe and Megan Parker for your work on such beautiful and vivid illustrations. You are crucial!

Enjoyed *The Outsider?*

Turn the page for a sample of

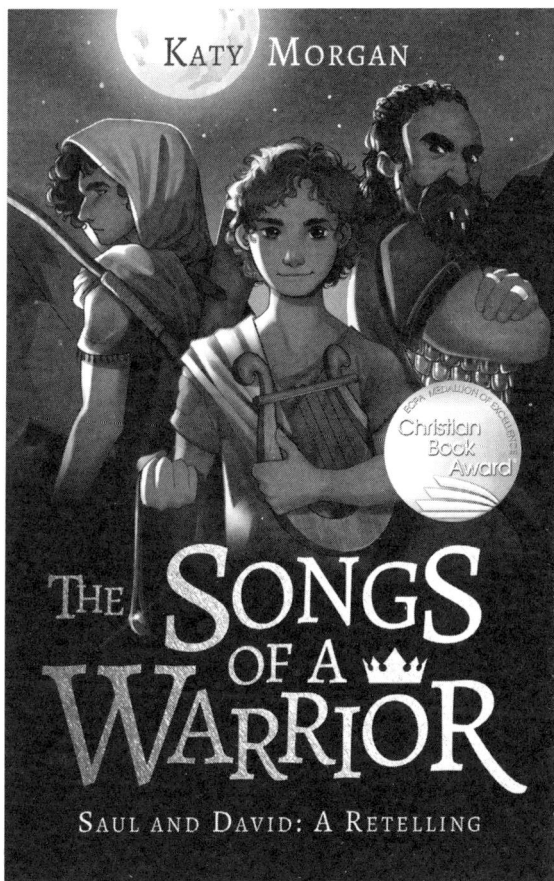

KATY MORGAN

THE SONGS OF A WARRIOR

SAUL AND DAVID: A RETELLING

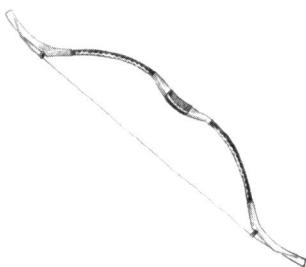

CHAPTER 1

The Boy with the Bow

There was a rock-dove in the tree. It was plump and purplish and looking happily away into the distance.

The boy on the ground beneath it was slowly raising his bow and carefully sliding an arrow out of his quiver.

Gently, Jonathan, he told himself, keeping his eyes fixed on the dove. He did feel a little sorry for it as it ruffled its feathers in a self-satisfied sort of way and clicked its beak. Poor silly bird. At least its last hour had been a happy one.

The arrow was out. He notched its feathered end to the bowstring.

Jonathan had made this bow himself, and it was a good one. It was small, just a hunting bow, not as big as the ones you'd use in battle. He had been practising with his grandfather's old war-bow but he couldn't bend it far enough to shoot it—not yet. But this one was just right.

His feet were firm. His hands were steady. He closed one eye and drew the arrow back...

Then, suddenly, the moment was lost. Somewhere behind Jonathan a sheep bleated. All at once the rockdove panicked and took off in a flurry of feathers.

Not its last hour, after all.

Jonathan groaned. Where had a *sheep* appeared from? Now he would have to go home empty-handed!

He turned round. There were three of them, all craggy old ewes with soft muzzles and dirty fleeces. They looked at him indignantly as if he had no right to be there.

Jonathan looked at them back. "You're in *my* way, I'm not in yours," he said.

He wondered who they belonged to. It would be odd to bring sheep into the woods deliberately. Had they got lost? They must have come up the hill... He'd better chase them back that way.

He had time. His grandfather Kish had said they had to leave for Mizpah at noon, and judging by the sun he wasn't late yet.

His stomach squirmed. Today was the day! He'd been looking forward to the assembly at Mizpah for weeks. And now, at last, the day had come when—

But Jonathan's thoughts were interrupted by a shout. Someone was calling out for help. Someone at the bottom of the hill, beyond the edge of the wood.

Without hesitating, Jonathan ran at the sheep, waving his bow in the air. "Yah!"

They jerked back, then lowered their heads and thundered away downhill. One of them almost got caught by the lower branches of a thorn tree, but she shook herself loose and followed her companions.

Jonathan followed too. His eyes took a moment to adjust to the sunlight as he left the wood, but soon he was watching the sheep race down to the valley-bottom—and there was the boy who'd shouted. He was still shouting, and waving frantically. He was about Jonathan's age and he had two more sheep at his heels.

What had happened? Jonathan set off running down the hill, sending small rocks tumbling as he did. He jumped from side to side to avoid them, took on speed, skidded down the last steep slope, and arrived at the bottom with a heaving chest and a wide grin on his face. He liked running.

But the shepherd boy wasn't smiling. "Did you see them?" he said urgently. "Did you see where they went?"

"Who? The sheep?"

"The thieves." The boy's dirty face was streaked with tears. "My master will kill me—they're all gone—some men came and took them—I couldn't stop them—but I can't go home with just five sheep—"

"Don't worry," Jonathan interrupted gently. "Those three were up in the wood. Maybe others will have escaped as well. Is this the direction the thieves came in? How long ago did they take them?"

"Not too long. Maybe half an hour ago." The boy was

calming down. He focused on Jonathan, grasping his arm. "You're Kish's grandson, aren't you? Can you help me? I'm Oren. I'm only a shepherd but—" His eyes were pleading and eager.

"I'll help," Jonathan said. Then he hesitated, glancing up at the sky. "But I've got to go soon. We're going to Mizpah."

"To the assembly!" Oren's eyes widened. "Then you'd better not help me. You can't be late for that. Not when…"

It was too huge a thing to say out loud. But Jonathan finished the other boy's sentence in his own head. *Not when God is going to choose a king for us.*

He looked at the sky again. It wasn't noon yet. "I have time," he decided. "A bit, anyway."

Oren nodded, suddenly becoming businesslike. "If I keep these five together, will you run ahead? Look for the others? You're a good runner."

Jonathan grinned—and sprinted away at full speed. His sandals left clouds of dust behind him.

But he didn't find any of the other sheep.

"Maybe they'll just wander home," he told Oren encouragingly as the two of them trailed back towards the town. "Some of our donkeys went missing a couple of months ago, and *they* returned."

"But your donkeys weren't stolen, were they?" said Oren gloomily. "They just got loose. I heard about it." He kicked at the dust.

Briefly Jonathan wondered what Oren had heard about the donkeys. His father, Saul, had gone to find them, but they'd wandered back while he was gone. Kish had raged, "That useless son of mine! He's probably halfway to Jabesh Gilead by now, and all the time the stupid donkeys were under his nose!"

Jonathan's cheeks went pink as he remembered. It wasn't a good feeling, thinking your father might be useless.

"My master will kill me," said Oren. "He hits me when I mess up just *small* things."

At that Jonathan forgot his father and grandfather. He wished he and Oren had been able to find the sheep. Fiercely, he said, "This is why we need a king. *He'd* stop people stealing and—and people beating up their servants."

"Maybe," replied Oren dully.

They'd reached the edge of Gibeah. Jonathan squeezed Oren on the arm, and the other boy trudged disconsolately away.

Jonathan followed the opposite path, looping around the low flat hill that supported the main part of the town. In front of him lay his grandfather's fields: they were bare and brown at the moment, ready for ploughing. Then there was the house, and the green rolling hills, with Kish's sheep grazing on them. Jonathan smiled contentedly as the sun found its way through a crack in the clouds and filled the valley with brilliant colour.

Then he gasped, and broke into a run. The sun! It was past noon! He was going to be late.

👑

He got away with just a raised eyebrow from Kish, who was standing impressively outside the house, his arms folded over his thick sheepskin coat. Abner was next to him, equally broad-chested but brown-haired instead of grey. Abner was Saul's cousin, Kish's nephew.

Jonathan's father, Saul, came out of the house. His tall frame was swaddled in a cloak, the richest one he had. There was fur sewn round its neck. He had put oil in his hair and rings on his fingers. "Jonathan," he exclaimed, "you're here at last." His eyes slid uncertainly to Kish. "You're late."

Kish said nothing, so Saul didn't say anything else either. A servant came round the house with the donkeys, and Jonathan hurried inside to get changed. He had to wear a heavy coat like his grandfather's, which he could already tell was going to be itchy and too hot. He had an embroidered cap over his hair and proper boots instead of sandals. His sister Merab handed him a thin gold ring: "Grandfather told me to give it to you. Now that you're one of the men."

Her voice was sarcastic, but Jonathan ignored that. She was right: he was one of the men now, going with his father and grandfather to represent their family and clan and tribe at the great gathering of all Israel. Right now it was the house of Kish, and then it would be the house of Saul, but one day people would talk about the house of Jonathan, who was not only an excellent hunter but also owned hundreds of sheep, and treated all his shepherds with respect.

Or, he thought excitedly, *Jonathan, the right-hand man of the king, the king God chose, the one who rules over all twelve tribes of Israel.*

He slid the ring onto his finger. It was too big, but he didn't let Merab see.

Outside again, the donkeys had been spread with fine fabrics and leather saddlebags. Mizpah was close enough that they could have walked there, but that would have looked cheap and unimpressive. They were going to take donkeys, and five servants, and everyone would know that the house of Kish was one of the best families in the whole tribe of Benjamin.

Michal, Jonathan's other sister, had twined herself around Saul's arm. "When will you be back?" she asked. "You were gone for ages and ages last time."

Saul shook her off. "Soon," he said, and climbed onto his donkey.

Michal transferred herself to Jonathan. She was six years younger than him and much skinnier; her bony arms clung tightly around his waist.

Jonathan squeezed her back. "See you later," he whispered, bending to touch the top of her head with his chin. "I can't wait to tell you all about it."

Her dark head nodded, and she stood back, letting him get onto his donkey.

"Ready?" growled Kish.

"Let's go," answered Saul.

Buy the award-winning *The Songs of a Warrior* at
www.thegoodbook.com/songs-of-a-warrior
www.thegoodbook.co.uk/songs-of-a-warrior

thegoodbook
COMPANY

BIBLICAL | RELEVANT | ACCESSIBLE

At The Good Book Company we are dedicated to helping Christians and local churches grow. We believe that God's growth process always starts with hearing clearly what he has said to us through his timeless and flawless word—the Bible.

Ever since we opened our doors in 1991, we have been striving to produce resources that are biblical, relevant, and accessible. By God's grace, we have grown to become an international publisher, encouraging ordinary Christians of every age and stage and every background and denomination to live for Christ day by day and equipping churches to grow in their knowledge of God, their love for one another, and the effectiveness of their outreach.

Call one of our friendly team for a discussion of your needs or visit one of our local websites for more information on the resources and services we provide.

Your friends at The Good Book Company

thegoodbook.com | thegoodbook.co.uk
thegoodbook.com.au | thegoodbook.co.nz
thegoodbook.co.in